THE UNOFFICIAL COLLEGE GUIDE TO YALE WITH MURDER

Other Ivy League Murder Mysteries
from SparkCollege:

The Unofficial Guide to Harvard . . . with Murder!

THE UNOFFICIAL COLLEGE GUIDE TO YALE WITH MURDER

OR...EVERYTHING YOU EVER WANTED TO KNOW ABOUT YALE BUT WERE TOO ~~AFRAID~~ DEAD TO ASK.

SPARKCOLLEGE
AN IMPRINT OF SPARK PUBLISHING

WWW.SPARKCOLLEGE.COM

This book has not been endorsed by Yale University. All descriptions of Yale and opinions about Yale are solely the views of the authors. This is a work of fiction. All names, characters, incidents, and dialogue are imaginary, and any resemblance to persons living or deceased is entirely coincidental.

Written by Matthew Belinkie and Jordan Stokes.

© 2006 by Spark Publishing

All rights reserved. No part of this publication may be reproduced, stored in a retrieval system, or transmitted, in any form or by any means, electronic, mechanical, photocopying, recording, or otherwise, without prior written permission from the publisher.

SparkCollege is an imprint of SparkNotes LLC

Spark Publishing
A Division of Barnes & Noble
120 Fifth Avenue
New York, NY 10011
www.sparknotes.com

ISBN-13: 978-1-4114-9869-3
ISBN-10: 1-4114-9869-0

Library of Congress Cataloging-in-Publication Data

Unofficial college guide to Yale—with murder : everything you ever wanted to know about Yale but were too dead to ask.
    p. cm.
  1. Yale University   Fiction. 2. New Haven (Conn.)   Fiction. 3. College students   Fiction. 4. College stories.

PS3600.A1U56 2006
813'.6   dc22

                                                                2006023735

Please submit changes or report errors to www.sparknotes.com/errors.

Printed and bound in the United States.

1 3 5 7 9 10 8 6 4 2

Acknowledgments

Our heartfelt thanks go out to:

Jessica Johnson, Shana Mlawski, and Brian Tippy, for their long hours and keen insight.

Olga Berlinsky, Carlos Hann, Alexandria Lefkovits, Jon Markman, Nicholas Seaver, Larry Wise, and Zachary Zwillinger, for catching (at least some of) our embarrassing mistakes.

All those who were there to answer our questions, especially Christina Agapakis, Nick Baumann, Mike Chan, Neil Chatani, Ronli Diakow, Veronique Greenwood, Chris Hudson, Alice Jones, Doug London, Iris Ma, Leslie Root, Errol Saunders, and Matt Wrather.

"Peter Fenzel," "Jeremiah Quinlan," "Ryan Sheely," "Gary Puhlman," "Josh McNeil" and "Jessica Shechner," who are entirely fictional and not based on any real person, living or dead, we promise.

The Progressive Party, the *Rumpus*, the Fifth Humour, the men of Lawrance Hall suite A12, and the Yale Precision Marching Band, just for doing the things they do.

Maureen and the rest of the gang at SparkNotes, for putting up with our flagrant abuse of the word count.

And finally, two special shoutouts: one from Jordan to Tomomi Mimura for her unswerving support (*and* for her insight, *and* for catching mistakes, *and* for her last-minute cameo appearance), and one from Matt to Oliver Kettleson-Belinkie, Yale class of 2027.

Introduction

What you are about to read is not real . . . well, there's no real murder, anyway.

What is real is the information about Yale. This story is stuffed with need-to-know facts, large and small, about all things **Eli**. Our crack team of Yalies have given up their hard-won knowledge and infused it into a murder mystery.

As you read the story, you'll notice that that Yale-related terms are defined in red along the sides of the pages. These nuggets of solid gold will tell you all about the ins and outs of choosing classes, feeding yourself, surviving the punishing workload, choosing the right fit among the **1,001 a cappella group**, finding the best parties, mocking Harvard properly, and maybe even finding some sweet Eli love.

Eli: Here's your first fact: Yalies are called Elis (ee-lies), after Elihu Yale, Yale's first benefactor. See page 58 for details.

1,001 a cappella: It's not quite that many, but there are a lot. Yale is swarming with singers. You'll need to know your Whiffenpoofs from your Spizzwinks. Trust us.

And whether you want to find out more about the school before you apply, or you just want to avoid embarrassing freshman year mistakes, don't miss these vital nuggets of Yale love:

Most Popular Majors: ... and Their Stereotypes 11
Off-Campus: New Haven's Non-Yale Claims to Fame..... 21
Yale Unveiled: Cool Places at Yale You Probably
    Won't Be Allowed to Go 45
Drink Up!: New Haven Coffee Shops.................... 53
Shop Till You Drop: Shopping Period Strategies.......... 61
Residential Colleges................................... 75
Know Your Dans 97
Really Off-Campus: Sketchy New Haven Places to Go ... 109
Party Time: Species of Yale Party 123
Go Back to the Yahd: Why Yale Is Better
    Than Harvard 131
Yale Myths Debunked: Yale Myths, or "Lies My Tour
    Guide Told Me" 139

CHAPTER
One

It's amazing how back in high school we all managed to get up at seven o'clock. The only reason Yalies will be up at that hour is if they're finishing a paper or making the walk of shame. It leads to some interesting meetings on the sidewalk.

My alarm went off at ten thirty that Wednesday morning, but it felt like five thirty (maybe because I'd been up playing pool till four thirty). I keep the alarm on the far side of the room, which makes it more difficult to roll over, hit the snooze, and go back to sleep. But because the bulk of my possessions live in a series of broad, sloping piles on the floor, my first few seconds of wakefulness are always a painful steeplechase over clothes, books, and the occasional half-empty pizza box.

I went over to my dresser and pounded the buzzer into submission. There was just enough time to shower and get to class, but I couldn't resist flopping into my desk chair and checking my email first. There was the usual stuff—the **Master**'s office

Master: A professor who lives in the residential college, along with spouse, children, and pets. One of the Master's main duties is setting up "Teas." These are held in the Master's living room, with students balancing tea and cookies on their laps and listening to the former head of the CIA talk about ordering Khrushchev killed (or something).

> **Dramat:** All the Dramat productions have big budgets, large crews (up to forty undergrads working behind the scenes), access to the Drama School's props and costumes, and, most important, they get to use the swanky Drama School Theater. There's also a lot of non-Dramat theater at Yale. Complaining about how the Dramat hogs all the resources is a major cottage industry.
>
> **Progressive Party:** One of the six parties of the Yale Political Union. The members of these groups socialize, debate, and drink, the relative emphasis of the three varying from group to group. The Progs . . . well, they debate some. Many Yalies who aren't in the YPU think of it as an insignificant ball of hot gas, but remember: there's been at least one Yalie in the running for president or vice president in every election since 1972.

was offering cheap tickets to a show in New York, I had an invitation to a cast party for the **Dramat**'s production of *Our Town*, and someone had been foolish enough to start a gun-control debate on the **Progressive Party** discuss list, which had yielded a deluge of responses. Then I noticed a message from Jeremiah Quinlan, the professor of my Eighteenth-Century Fiction and Society course. The subject line read "Your paper." The message was simply: "Mr. Bowman: Come see me at office hours. Bring your source material."

Quinlan's office hours were now. This meant getting dressed. I had a quick look in the mirror to survey the damage. It wasn't too extensive—I still looked like the guy listed as Miles Bowman on my driver's license. My short, way-too-curly hair hadn't thinned an inch. Eyes still green, as listed, but a bit puffier than normal. All six feet of me were still intact, though undressed. I fumbled around and found a pair of jeans under a pile of books and a heavy cable-knit sweater sticking out of my gym bag. The first pair of shoes I laid eyes on were an embarrassing bright red pair of Pumas, but they would have to do. I needed to be swift. Swift like a cat.

Pulling my secondhand overcoat tightly around my shoulders in a futile attempt to seal out the November wind, I considered the meaning of the message. *I read your paper*, I thought sourly. *Was it "I read your very good paper," or "I read your bad paper, which will receive an F"?*

Quinlan was a **Berkeley Fellow**. His office was in the college. To get to his office, I cut across the grass of **Cross Campus**. Not that there was much grass left after a semester of hard-fought soccer and Frisbee games. Ahead of me was **Sterling Memorial Library**, with its cathedral-like entrance dwarfed by fourteen stories of book stacks. New England winters had left black streaks down the gray stone, which matched the overcast sky perfectly. Yale seemed built with the winter in mind, unlike my coat. I shivered and hurried toward Berkeley.

Another student was waiting outside the office when I got there. Jessica Shechner was a senior in Silliman. I'd gone to a party in her suite during **Camp Yale** when I was a frosh and she had tried to sell me on the sciences. I'd been a little in awe of her at the time, so it had been a bit unnerving to wind up in Dr. Quinlan's seminar with her.

Berkeley Fellow: There are three different types of fellows: (1) Grad students, who help plan social events and tutor; (2) professors, who arrange talks and dispense advice; and (3) celebrities that have little or nothing to do with Yale. (For instance, Martha Stewart is a Stiles Fellow.)

Cross Campus: The central lawn of the university. Like the National Mall, except instead of a reflecting pool you get lots of grass, which is a lot more useful anyway.

Sterling Memorial Library: Yale's main library, the largest open-stack library in the world. This means you go into the stacks yourself to find books, which is kind of cool, but kind of a pain in the neck, since it's the largest open-stack library in the world.

Camp Yale: Camp Yale is the period between when students arrive on campus in August and when classes actually start. It's one glorious final burst of summer vacation before you actually need to unpack your alarm clock. Every organization sets up an information table at a massive "extracurricular bazaar" in a desperate attempt to recruit new blood.

"Hey Bowman," she said, nodding at me.

"Jess," I said, sitting on the wooden bench beside her. "What drags you away from your **gels**?"

"Trying to get an early start on my last English assignment at Yale," she said happily. "Once my Humanities requirement is out of the way, I'll never have to leave **Science Hill** again. So what are you doing here?"

"Quinlan wants to see me about last week's paper."

"Uh-oh. Any idea why?"

I sighed. "Possibly because I wrote it on a jokebook."

The assignment had been to analyze a minor eighteenth-century novel. I'd gone to **Mudd Library** to find something particularly minor and had come across a slim red book calling out from between two immense brown volumes, like a thong rising jauntily out of a pair of low-rider jeans. On its spine, in thin gold letters, was written, *The Philogelos, or, The Laughter Lover*. It turned out not to be a novel at all, but rather a translation of an ancient Greek jokebook that had ended up in the wrong section of the library.

---

gels: A component in many science experiments. Damned if we know what the hell they are, but Bio majors seem to spend most of their waking hours waiting for a gel to "run" or complaining about how much time they spend waiting for gels to run.

Science Hill: The area to the north of central campus with all the science buildings. Yalies love to complain about the walk, even though it's ten minutes tops, and the "Hill" thing is a bit of an exaggeration. The school is in the middle of a $500 million renovation of the science facilities (which, considering the price, presumably includes the installation of solid-gold desks).

Mudd Library: The books from all of Yale's libraries that never get used eventually get carted away to the appropriately named Mudd Library Annex (located next to the graveyard, also appropriately). It's not unusual to find a book there that hasn't been checked out since the Civil War.

I'd taken it out of curiosity along with a few different novels, and I'd joked to my friends that since it had been translated in the eighteenth century, maybe I could use it for the assignment. The thing was, none of the novels inspired me, and the deadline was bearing down relentlessly. With days to go—confronted with three papers, a midterm, and bronchitis, and half-hallucinating from a combination of NyQuil and DayQuil—I had the option of quitting all my **extracurriculars** or phoning in the paper. I succumbed to desperation and churned out fifteen pages on how a translation of a jokebook is kind of like a novel. Sort of.

"A *jokebook*?" echoed Jessica, her eyes wide.

"Yeah. I thought I'd be a campus legend—like that guy who wrote his **senior essay** on 'Cold War Themes in *Rocky IV*.' Instead, I'll be that guy who flunked English."

She patted my arm encouragingly. "Don't be so dramatic. Worst case scenario, you'll get a **B–**. By the way," she added, "do you have the book on you? This I gotta see."

Professor Quinlan's office door opened suddenly and his disheveled head of gray

extracurriculars: Yalies like to keep busy. Freshmen usually join as many extracurriculars as they can handle and probably a few more. By sophomore or junior year, most Yalies have cut it back to just one or two, but they're so deeply involved with these that it starts affecting their grades. There are hundreds of groups on campus, and new ones are formed every year. Other than residential colleges, extracurriculars are where you will make most of your friends.

senior essay: Most majors culminate in a senior essay, a huge paper that you work on with one-on-one guidance from the professor of your choice. The best thing about senior essays is that in April, Rudy's (a local dive bar) puts up a clothesline, and seniors are invited to hang their title pages on it for a free drink.

B–: Every paper you write in English, history, or poli-sci will get something between an A and a B–. That is, unless your TA is waging a one-man war on grade inflation, in which case most papers will get a C. Note that the number of TAs waging one-man wars on grade inflation is higher than you might expect.

hair poked out. He was wearing a tweed blazer with suede patches and a bowtie. He always looked like he'd stepped out of *Academic Stereotype Quarterly*.

"Jessica was here before me," I offered quickly.

"No no, Miles, you first," he said, lighting up his pipe. "I'm very excited about your paper!"

"Really? Uh, I mean, great! Me too," I said, rather lamely. As Quinlan pulled me into the office by a sleeve, I caught a glimpse of Jessica staring after us with a dark expression that seemed to say, "I can't wait to get back to **KBT**."

"Thank you for coming so quickly, Miles," said Professor Quinlan, sitting down in his desk chair.

"No problem," I said, sliding into the chair across from him.

"Always say 'You're welcome,'" he corrected me. "'No problem' implies that had it been a problem, you would not have done it."

"Yes, sir."

"I read your paper last night, and I wanted to tell you right away that you did a fantastic job."

"Really?" I said again. I was going to have to buy more DayQuil.

"In fact," he said, "I may nominate it for the **Betts Prize**."

"Oh! Uh, thank you! That's . . . really good."

"I'll just need to review the work more closely. That's why I requested that you bring the source material."

KBT: Klein Biology Tower, home of the Bio department, numerous labs, a science library, and the office of Nobel Laureate Sidney Altman. KBT also has its own dining hall, so the poor premeds never have an excuse to leave. On the bright side, it's got some of the best views in New Haven.

Betts Prize: Yale gives away a dizzying array of prizes each year, both through departments and through the residential colleges. They're usually created in memory of someone, so you may be surprised to learn that, for example, you've been chosen as the junior "who most closely approaches the standard of good scholarship and character set by Francis Gordon Brown . . . class of 1901."

"Absolutely!" I blurted. "Of course!" I went into my backpack quickly, worried that he might change his mind if I gave him a minute to think about it. He took the book, ran a finger over the gold letters on the spine, and placed it on his desk.

"Well now, Miles," he said briskly. "We can discuss your thesis later. For now, go and celebrate." He reached out and gave me a firm handshake. "Keep up the good work!"

Most Popular Majors

. . . and Their Stereotypes

Miles belongs to the very popular English department. Here's a bit more about the popular majors at Yale.

History

Yalies will tell you they're majoring in history, the biggest major, with a vaguely apologetic tone. A lot of people end up as history majors by default after failing to develop an interest more specific than "everything that's ever happened." Also a popular major for premeds who have given up pretending they like science. In any given Yale graduating class, there will be about five people who chose the history major because they actually care about the subject. They will all become professors.

Economics

There are two types of economics majors. First, there are the people who are double majoring in econ and poli-sci—the two easiest majors at Yale—and they love telling people with false modesty that "Yeah, I'm double majoring in econ and poli-sci, no biggy." They're in it for the money, and they know this is less pressure than medicine or law. They will be investment bankers for four years and then burn out. Then there are the people who, for some bizarre reason, actually love economics. They are dedicated to the principal that anything can be graphed and predicted. They don't care about making money, although they will. They will be investment bankers for four years and then burn out.

Political Science

Predictably, poli-sci majors feel very strongly about politics. On one side, you've got your angry liberals, people so liberal that they make normal liberals not want to be liberal anymore. On the other, you've got your angry conservatives, who wear ties to class and intern with the NRA. Rolling around the middle of this ideological Hungry Hungry Hippos board are the normal people, who usually try to jump ship to International Relations or the cool sounding "Ethics, Politics, and Economics," in which they might actually learn something useful and do some good.

English

At a university full of stellar departments, Yale's English department is acknowledged to be one of the best in the country, especially for undergrads. We even have living legend Harold Bloom, who publishes a book every four months and never stops rubbing his shoulder. If you believe that Salman Rushdie is just as good as Shakespeare, you'll probably be happier as a literature major. English is all about the good old dead white men

Biology

Biology is divided—between the people who actually want to be scientists and the premeds who are just out to get the highest grades they can and secretly hate science. The premeds hate the scientists because they actually care (and thus threaten to ruin the curve), and the scientists hate the premeds for being a bunch of science-hating grade whores. Since science majors take more of the exact same courses than humanities majors, they tend to be very cliquish.

American Studies

Traditionally, this is the "easy" major for dumb jocks who want to write their papers on the Real World/Road Rules Challenge. Actually, any major with *studies* in it will work pretty well for this.

Psychology

Psych majors take a couple of survey courses their freshman year and immediately start analyzing everyone they know. This lasts until approximately midway through junior year, at which point they switch gears and start complaining about how everyone who's taken Intro Psych thinks he's Sigmund freaking Freud.

CHAPTER
Two

I spent the day feeling pretty smart. My Skepticism Ancient and Modern seminar flew by in a daze. I emailed a **reading response** to my Ancient Persian History TA a full two hours early. I felt so damn smart, I would have dropped the **Credit/D/Fail** option for Drugs in American Culture, if it hadn't been past the deadline. I saw my future tagline: "Prize-winning Miles Bowman, up-and-coming young scholarly powerhouse."

On my way back from the movies much later in the day, I saw the red and blue strobes of police cars lighting up the walls of Saybrook. I hurried along High Street to join a big crowd gathered around the base of **Harkness Tower**. An acquaintance of mine, Emily, was snapping

reading response: To make sure you aren't completely blowing off the reading, some professors require you to do a weekly essay of a few hundred words.

Credit/D/Fail: If you take a course Credit/D/Fail, any grade of a C– or higher is recorded as "Credit" and not factored into your GPA. This encourages transcript-conscious students to loosen up and try something new. You can change your mind and decide to take a grade up until mid-term, in case you turn out to be better at Middle English than you thought.

Harkness Tower: Yale's most prominent landmark, a 216-foot-tall faux-Gothic tower. It houses the Yale Memorial Carillon, which is played at noon and five.

CHAPTER TWO | 16

pictures of the crowd. I remembered that she was a photographer for **Rumpus**.

"Hey," I said. "What's going on?"

"Somebody jumped."

"Who was it?"

"Some professor, I think. I didn't catch the name. Vineland? Quinby?"

With a knot forming in my stomach, I pushed myself to the front of the crowd and pressed against the police tape cordoning off a twenty-foot stretch of pavement. It was him all right. His yellow, green, and red **J. Press** scarf was draped with incongruous elegance over his body, slowly absorbing the surprisingly small pool of blood. My first thought, I'm sorry to admit, was to wonder whether he'd nominated my paper for the Betts Prize before killing himself.

As I stared at the body, I overheard a gruff-voiced man saying, "Did he seem depressed recently?"

"Don't waste your time looking for a note," came the reply. "There's no way he killed himself."

I looked over toward the **Branford Gate** to see a mustachioed detective interrogating an indignant, tiny girl in a Yale sweatshirt. The girl was somewhere between very cute and beautiful, with a

---

Rumpus: "The Only Magazine at Yale about Stuff at Yale." *Rumpus* is the nation's first college tabloid, printing the important stories about drunk frat boys getting arrested, Secret Society initiation rituals, students working as strippers, and exactly how much toilet paper it takes to clog a Yale toilet. (A freaking ton, as it happens. Those things are like fire hoses.)

J. Press: A hoity-toity menswear store, founded in 1902, which has become much less popular since Yalies stopped wearing suits to class. It is kept in business through brisk sales of patterned scarves—there's a different one for every residential college and every political party in the YPU.

Branford Gate: Technically the Harkness Memorial Gate. They say if you walk through it, you'll never graduate. This isn't much of an issue since it's always closed and locked (except during commencement). Wide enough to drive an Escalade through, the pointed archway is dripping with sculpted figures representing every field of human endeavor. It's a perfect example of Yale architecture—gorgeous, insanely detailed, and largely ignored by the students.

heart-shaped face and chin-length red hair that couldn't quite decide whether it was curly or frizzy. She looked like she had escaped from a screwball comedy from the silent era—bobbed hair, a little bow of a mouth, a smattering of golden freckles high on her cheekbones, and deep brown eyes as large as a deer's.

To my surprise, I realized I knew her—well, sort of. Her name was Nina. About a month ago, I had been talking to Professor Quinlan during office hours when she'd entered the room to place a stack of photocopies on his desk. He'd mumbled an introduction and she glanced at me, and I instantly forgot what we were talking about. She struck me then the same way that she struck me now. I had stared at her, mesmerized, until she turned to leave, breaking our momentary eye contact. I went to office hours again the following week in the hopes of running into her, but she never showed up. Instead, Quinlan and I had spent an hour talking about how Kipling was an underrated poet and *Moll Flanders* was the worst book in the English language. Even though I'd kept my eyes peeled for her, I'd never seen her since. Back in the present, the detective sighed loudly. "Listen, miss, why don't you leave this to us?" he asked.

"You didn't know him! He was the happiest guy I ever met!" Nina insisted.

"Yeah?" The detective took a long look at the professor's body. "I've seen happier."

She turned her head away in exasperation, and our eyes met. Normally I'd have looked away, but her eyes had a way of making me forget to be shy. Especially now, when tears were forming at the corners of her eyes. I took a half step forward, wanting to do something to comfort her, before I remembered that she didn't even know me. I was about to turn away, when I saw her mouth the word "Help" in my direction. I looked over my shoulder to see whom she was talking to, then realized it was me. I took a deep breath and ducked under the police tape without another thought.

"Now," the detective was saying, "can you please tell me what time the professor normally . . ."

"Excuse me, Officer. I'm her **freshman counselor**," I lied, trying to look older than I was. "Nina seems a little shaken up. Can I take her home?"

Don't ask me her last name, I prayed to myself. *Don't ask me her last name!*

He scowled at me and then waved us off with his pen. "An officer's waiting to search Quinlan's office for a note. Once she unlocks the door for us, she's free to go."

I led her through the crowd. "Thank you," she said, sniffling. "If I'd stayed there much longer I would have ended up assaulting an officer of the law."

"I know the feeling. I almost decked the **fire marshal** my freshman year when he fined us for 'excess clutter.'"

Nina laughed. It was a damn fine-sounding laugh.

---

freshman counselor: A freshman counselor (or "froco") is a senior in the same college as her frosh, who lives on the Old Campus with the freshmen. She organizes social events, gives advice of all sorts, and sometimes is just there as a shoulder to cry on. What she is *not* is a narc—freshmen counselors will almost always let their charges party their little hearts out. However, at least one froco is on duty every Thursday, Friday, and Saturday night, in case someone needs to be rushed to the hospital or stabbed with an adrenaline needle like in *Pulp Fiction*.

fire marshal: The fire marshal can enter your room while you're out and fine you for owning hotplates and tapestries. The good news is that anything covered, he can't uncover, so if you get word that the marshal's on the prowl and throw a towel over your microwave (yes, microwaves are against the rules) you'll be okay.

CHAPTER TWO

"I'm Miles Bowman," I said. "I'm in—was in the professor's Eighteenth Century Fiction and Society class."

"Nina Lennox." Suddenly her brow furrowed. "I guess you already knew that, huh?"

"Professor Quinlan told me who you were."

"When you saw me at his office hours that one time, right?" she said, visibly reassured. I couldn't help feeling excited that she remembered me, too.

We hurried across Elm Street, barely avoiding the **cars**, and she fell in beside me. I had to shove my hands in my pockets to stop myself from throwing an arm around her.

"You were close to Quinlan?" I asked.

She sighed. "Not really. He was an old friend of my father's, and he sort of took me under his wing when I got here, but . . . really, I've only known him for a few months. Still . . ."

"Yeah. Still."

We followed the **Rose Walk** in silence past Trumbull College out onto Cross Campus. Glancing up at the imposing bulk of Sterling Library, I remembered something and frowned. "Um, Nina?"

cars: It's a miracle that students aren't flattened daily on Elm Street. The townies drive like maniacs and the Yalies are too impatient to wait for a red light. It's like Frogger out there. And don't even think of setting foot on Prospect Street without wearing a helmet.

Rose Walk: The brick walkway connecting Elm Street and Cross Campus. It's named after a donor, so don't go looking for actual roses.

"Yes?" she said. She stopped and looked right at me. Under normal circumstances, I might have realized what I was about to say was insensitive. But I was looking right into those eyes again, and it completely shut down my brain.

"As long as you're heading to Quinlan's office right now," I blurted, "the professor has a library book of mine." I could see her expression hardening with every word that came out of my mouth. "It's, um, going to be overdue soon," I added weakly, "so if you could just grab it, I'd—"

"You know what?" she interrupted, in a tired voice. "I think I can take it from here. Thanks again for the rescue. I'll make sure you get your book."

She headed off toward Berkeley alone without waiting for a response. I slumped back up **Broadway**, dragged my books to **Stiles Library**, and tried to lose myself in work. Although I was there until the wee hours as usual, it didn't make me feel any smarter. *Goodbye, Professor Quinlan,* I thought. *Goodbye, Betts Prize. Goodbye, Nina.*

Broadway: The main retail strip of the campus. Most of the real estate is owned by the university, which has been trying to turn Broadway into Harvard Square by bringing in national chains like Urban Outfitters, Origins, and J. Crew. The street certainly looks very clean (which one supposes was more or less the point), but most Yalies can't afford to shop at these places.

Stiles Library: No one in history has ever actually tried to find a book in a residential college library. The shelves could be stuffed with porn and the student body would never realize. But the convenience of a 24-hour quiet space 30 seconds from your room makes them popular destinations for intense study sessions.

Off-Campus

New Haven's Non-Yale Claims to Fame

Yale isn't the only thing that makes New Haven famous. Check it out.

Knights of Columbus headquarters
A Catholic organization in the vein of the Elks or the Stonecutters, it boasts 1.6 million members worldwide. The glass tower with a huge pillar at each corner is one of New Haven's most distinctive buildings, which is saying something.

Firsts
Louis' Lunch claims to have invented the hamburger, and Pepe's claims to have invented the pizza. More important, in 1908 George C. Smith of New Haven put sticks into balls of candy and named the treat after his favorite racehorse: "Lolly Pop." Other New Haven inventions: the cotton gin, the revolver, the Frisbee, the wireless radio, and the indoor mall.

IKEA
In 2004, IKEA opened its first store in New England at Long Wharf, drawing 20,000 people on the first day. Many a freshman suite has bonded over picking out a coffee table here. If you're really cheap, you can go to the Salvation Army and buy used IKEA furniture, which smells faintly of human misery.

Regicides of Charles I fled here

Three of the judges that sentenced Charles I of England to die during Cromwell's Puritan Revolution fled to New Haven after the Restoration. The "hanging judges" were named Whalley, Dixwell, and Goff. Stand outside the Yale bookstore and look north to see their other outstanding contribution to history. Or just MapQuest© it.

CHAPTER
Three

"If he wanted to kill himself, fine," said the Puh, taking a bite of pizza. "What offends me is how he had to do it in a way that embarrassed Yale. It's not right."

"I have no idea," I said. "You gonna finish those fries?"

We sat together at an immense wooden table in **Commons**. Quinlan's face stared out from hundreds of copies of the **YDN** strewn on every table. It was a terrible picture, as if the professor were reacting to the headline above him: "Beloved Lit Professor Kills Self in Bizarre Tower Dive."

"I don't buy the suicide angle," the Puh said, in between gulps of bright blue punch. "Why would a Yale professor kill himself? I mean, a professor! With tenure! At Yale! *Yale*, Miles!"

I ignored this. I knew from experience that Gary's uncanny zeal for all things

Commons: The main dining hall for undergrads, a huge building with stern-looking portraits of dead white men on the walls and a comically large Yale banner hanging from the far end.

YDN: Available for free in the dining halls five days a week, the *Yale Daily News* is required reading for every Yalie. Also required: complaining about the typos, the amount of the paper taken directly from the press wires, and the occasional photo caption that reads "CAPTION GOES HERE." Still, a daily newspaper, completely student run . . . pretty impressive. And it's a good makeshift umbrella if you get caught in the rain.

DS: Directed Studies (aka "Directed Suicide"). A program for freshmen that dare to drink from the fire hose of the Western canon. It consists of three full-year classes in literature, history, and philosophy, from the ancient Greeks to the nineteenth century. A five-page paper is due every Friday, and, fiendishly, there's a lecture that morning, during which everyone falls asleep.

YCC: Yale College Council. The student government of Yale. It's only slightly more effectual than your high school student council. Its members always have plans to change the world and in 2006 won a major victory when the university agreed to start providing soap in the bathrooms. But to most students, the YCC's one job is to find a bitchin' band for Spring Fling. Last year, only 20 percent of the student body bothered to vote in the YCC elections, even though it takes only a minute to do so online.

without blinking: This might seem perfectly normal, but in fact a lot of Yalies are hesitant about telling people where they go to school. "Dropping the Y-bomb" (as it's called) can engender everything from an awkward pause to awe to outright resentment. To avoid these reactions, some Yalies just say, "I go to school in Connecticut."

Stiles Dean: It's your residential college Dean's job to make sure you graduate. He has to approve your schedule, so if you want to double major in Zulu and painting, you're going to have to sell it to him first.

Yale was incurable and untreatable. I'd met Gary Puhlman (or the Puh, as he was universally known) in **DS** last year, and we had become fast friends while pulling all-nighters every Thursday. Gary was a religious man, and his religion was Yale. He went to all the sporting events (even field hockey) and he was a representative to the **YCC**. He was the kind of guy who, when asked by a stranger where he went to school, would reply "Yale!" **without blinking**.

"Anyway," he said, "what's going to happen to your class?"

"I talked to the **Stiles Dean**," I told him. "He says we can drop without penalty if we want, but they're going to find someone to teach the last week. It won't be the first time I've had my papers graded by a grad student."

"Hey! Yale has a student-to-teacher ratio of just seven to one! Furthermore—"

I quickly changed the subject. "So," I asked, "do you think I officially ruined things with Nina?"

"I have a theory," he said. "What if she really got mad at you for not making a move?"

"She seemed kind of traumatized. I don't think she was interested."

CHAPTER THREE

"You're a fine, upstanding Yale man; why shouldn't she be interested?"

"Gary, *every* man here is a Yale man! And a lot of us are single and lonely."

"Miles!" shouted a pleasant tenor. I winced slightly. It was my old suitemate, Paul. Paul Duffy was exactly the kind of guy you expected to meet at a place like Yale, although you were still shocked when you did. A **triple legacy**, he pulled straight As without breaking a sweat. He played varsity soccer. He sang in an **a cappella** group. He'd even made the **Beautiful People** issue of *Rumpus* as a freshman (leaning against a brick wall with his bowtie undone on page 18). I'd secretly nicknamed him "Perfect" Paul. He was rarely single and lonely.

He glided across Commons toward us. "Special delivery," he said, fishing a familiar red-bound volume out of his backpack. "Nina asked me to hand this to you." He patted me on the shoulder. "Good to see the old DS crew! Just like old times. Hey, when are we all going to get together for lunch?"

"Soon." I nodded. "Real soon. I'll call you. Hey . . . I didn't know you knew Nina." Maybe he could smooth things over with her.

triple legacy: You've heard the stories. And they're true, to an extent. You'll meet at least one person at Yale who's the great-great-great-great-great-grandnephew of Jonathan Edwards, or something like that. But legacy status isn't what it used to be—if it figures into the admissions process at all, it's only as a tie-breaker.

a cappella: With fourteen or so different groups, competition for the best singers can be fierce. You know how some schools have fraternity rush? Yale has an a cappella rush, which culminates in Tap Night in mid-September.

Beautiful People: *Rumpus*'s annual "50 Most Beautiful People" issue is always the subject of great anticipation and debate. The selection process is by no means scientific—*Rumpus* staffers basically make a list of their own crushes and poll their friends.

> **Beta:** One of Yale's fraternities. Greek life isn't as big a deal at Yale as it is at many other schools. The residential college system gives a lot of students all the sense of community that they need. Nevertheless the frat scene has been gradually becoming more popular, and Yale now has ten fraternities and three sororities. The parties are the bread and butter of some (mostly frosh). But rest assured: you won't feel pressure to join a fraternity, and you can have a great time at Yale without ever setting foot in one.
>
> **observatory:** STARRY, Yale's astronomy club, gets free run of the Leitner Observatory on the second and fourth Thursdays of every month, and it's open to the public on the first and third.
>
> **Bach Society:** In addition to the flagship Yale Symphony Orchestra, Yale has several other groups with which to get your viola on.
>
> **the Lizzie:** A private organization in a neat white house, the Elizabethan Club is dedicated to the appreciation of old English culture (because it's not like there's plenty of that at Yale anyway). Tea is the Lizzie's main draw. It offers a full tea service seven days a week during the school year to members (undergrads, grad students, and professors) and their guests. Want to join? Too bad. They only take a couple dozen people per class.

He blushed. "We're dating, actually."

"Awesome!" I blurted out, a little too loudly. "How did *that* happen?"

"I picked her up last month at that **Beta** party I invited you guys to."

"So," said Gary, "is this just a random hookup thing?"

"Oh no, I'm crazy about her. It got real intense real fast. I even met her folks during Parents Weekend." He looked around and leaned in. "Don't tell her, but I've been spending some time at the **observatory**, trying to discover something to name after her."

Of course, I thought. *She's a gorgeous premed, he's a humanities pretty boy. The perfect couple. They'll probably stay together forever and have lots of brilliant children with perfect teeth.*

"Anyway, I should be running on," said Paul. "I'm trying to slam out this little violin concerto in time for the next **Bach Society** concert."

"Good luck with that," I said with a forced smile.

"Call me," he said, pointing at us with a perfect finger. "We'll hit **the Lizzie**." He walked away, saying hi to about a dozen other people on his way to the door.

CHAPTER THREE

"Well," Gary said placidly, taking another bite of his pizza, "I have no idea what she sees in him."

I glowered at him and gathered my books. "I gotta run. Dean Sheely wants to talk to me about Professor Quinlan."

Gary looked up. "You're going to see Sheely?"

"Yeah. He called me this morning." Ryan Sheely was an associate dean of Student Affairs—someone you usually don't talk to unless you're in trouble. But since I hadn't pulled a giant condom over the **Morse lipstick** or anything, I'd assumed it had something to do with finding a replacement professor for my class. Looking at Gary's unhappy face, I began to worry. "What's wrong?" I asked.

"The guy has a bad reputation."

I looked at him seriously. "Gary, are you actually speaking ill of a Yale dean?"

"They say he hates undergrads." The Puh shrugged. "That's just what they say. I'm sure it's not true."

> **Morse lipstick:** One thing about the Morse lipstick is that it looks exactly like a . . . like something you'd put a giant condom on as a practical joke.

CHAPTER
Four

I walked into **Linsly-Chittenden Hall** and up the stairs to LC101, where Sheely was finishing up a class. I poked my head through the half-opened door of the classroom and examined him. Short and stout, he had a salt-and-pepper goatee that looked fake but probably wasn't, and he'd grown his remaining hair out to cover his baldness, which only made him look balder. He was gesturing at a slide of Humphrey Bogart with a pointer in a way that gave you the impression that he really enjoyed pointing at things.

Suddenly my phone rang, filling the room with the dulcet strains of "I'll Make Love to You." It sounded loud enough to be heard halfway to Pierson. Every head in the class turned toward me as I bolted back into the hall to answer it.

"Miles!" It was Nina.

Linsly-Chittenden Hall: A major classroom building located on the corner of Old Campus. Two things to note: first, Linsly-Chittenden also opens onto High Street, which makes it a useful shortcut. Second, no one ever calls this Linsly-Chittenden. Like most other Yale buildings it's just known by its initials: LC.

Facebook: The Facebook (.com) isn't officially affiliated with Yale, but they might as well name a residential college after it. A very popular site for students nationwide, it lets you create a profile for yourself and then spend all your free time looking at other people's profiles and building a completely pointless army of "Facebook friends." Most students have their profiles up before arriving on campus.

Hendrie: This is the headquarters of the symphony, the Glee Club, and the Yale bands (concert, jazz, and precision marching). Notoriously, it does not have an elevator, although the players of some of the heavier instruments have offered to pay for one themselves.

"Uh, hey." I somehow felt even more uncomfortable than I had a moment ago. "How'd you get my number?"

"I looked you up on **Facebook**," she said.

I wish I'd put a better picture up there, I thought.

"Did you return that book?" she asked urgently.

"Not yet." I cleared my throat. "Look, I wanted to apologize . . ."

"Listen! You can't return it yet!"

"Why not?" I asked.

"Miles, you have to promise me you won't show it to anyone before you talk to me!"

People started to file out of the classroom.

"Why?"

"Please?" she said in a pleading tone. "Just trust me."

Even if she *was* seeing Paul, there wasn't much resisting that voice.

"I promise," I told her.

"Thanks. I promise I'll explain everything. Meet me at **Hendrie** in an hour." And she hung up. I went back into the room, which was just about empty of students now. Sheely waved me over.

"Mr. Bowman! Thank you for the serenade from your pocket phone," he said, shuffling his notes into a satchel. I stood across the conference table from him and started to mumble a lame apology, but he cut me off.

"Professor Quinlan was a great friend of mine. We were undergrads here together. Do you know, Mr. Bowman, that when a Roman legionnaire died, his friends would fill the corpse with olive oil and float it down the Tiber?"

I considered this. "Really?" I asked in a tone of respectful skepticism.

He nodded. "Very good. That is, in fact, a complete lie. I make it a habit to tell one obvious lie whenever I meet someone new, so that I can see if that person trusts me implicitly. Which you obviously do not." Nothing in his tone of voice gave me any clue as to whether he was pleased at the outcome of his little experiment.

He leaned on the back of his chair. "You saw Professor Quinlan yesterday afternoon, is that correct?"

I nodded. "He didn't seem depressed, if that's what you wanted to know."

"I am not concerned with your insights into the human psyche, Mr. Bowman. What I would have from you is the subject of your conversation with dear Jeremiah, occurring as it did just hours before his last, long fall."

"My paper. He was going to nominate it for the Betts Prize," I said in the fleeting hope that Sheely might feel like honoring the dead man's wishes.

He gave me a level stare. "I mean to find out why my dear friend killed himself. I believe you undergrads value

Deans' Excuses: Deans have the awesome power to grant deans' excuses, which can absolve you of any deadline. Outside of murder mystery novels, these come from the residential college deans. Some will give them out like candy if you have a cold. Others need to see severed limbs. In any case, don't ask for too many, because someday you might really need one. Remember the story of the boy who cried SARS.

ExCom: The Executive Committee, where Yalies are sent when they've been naughty. Missteps include everything from tossing water balloons to plagiarism. It's extremely uncommon for a student to be expelled, or even suspended. The ExCom usually "reprimands" people, which means they wag a finger at you and send you away with a warning. That being said, it's still a name to reckon with.

DUH: Technically, this hospital on Hillhouse Avenue is now called University Health Services, but it's still widely referred to by its old name, DUH, for Department of Undergraduate Health. They'll give you a pregnancy test no matter what your complaint is, even if you're a guy.

Deans' Excuses above gold, do you not? You shall have them if you help me. But if I find out you know more than you are telling me today . . . you'll never see commencement. The road to **ExCom** is paved with bad intentions."

A part of me was shocked and offended by his bribe. But a much larger part of me was scared that he knew about the book in my backpack, and that this somehow meant I was in trouble. ExCom . . . I would have been happier if he'd threatened to send me to **DUH** with shattered kneecaps. But then I thought of Nina and my promise, and how she'd probably never speak to me again if I didn't keep it.

"Dean Sheely," I said. "I want to know what happened to the professor as much as anyone. If I think of anything you ought to know, I'll contact you."

He looked at me for a while. "That is all, for now," he said. "Good day."

CHAPTER
Five

Nina was waiting for me when I got to Hendrie, but she wouldn't say anything until we went to one of the **practice modules** on the top floor, closed the door, and pushed the upright piano against it.

"Okay," I said quietly, slouching uncomfortably into a folding chair. "I just lied to a powerful administrator on nothing more than your say-so. You need to explain, and fast." I was trying hard to be indignant and not be distracted by the way her hair just brushed the top of her collarbone.

She looked down at the linoleum for a moment. In the dim fluorescent light, her hair glowed a fiery red and her brown eyes deepened into such an intense chocolate color that I actually found myself staring

practice modules: Soundproofed capsules for musicians. Each residential college has at least one, and Hendrie has about a dozen.

at her open-mouthed for a moment. Fortunately, I caught myself before she looked up.

"Miles . . ." she began slowly. "I have proof that the professor was murdered."

I went cold. Someone in the next practice module was playing scales on the **Charles Ives Memorial Piano**. It sounded as uneasy as I felt.

She mutely handed me a sheet of paper. There was an email on it, addressed to her, from "anonymous.threatener235@gmail.com". It read: "Where is *The Philogelos?* Tell anyone about this message and you're next."

I looked at her, then back down at the piece of paper. Suddenly, having the piano pushed in front of the door didn't seem so silly.

"So," she said quietly, "you see why I need the book back."

I nodded. "You have to give this person whatever he wants."

She looked surprised. "No, I already replied and told him I have no idea what he's talking about."

"*What?*"

"I want to know what's so important about the book."

"You lied to the *murderer*? If you want to be a hero, then just tell the police and let them handle it!"

Charles Ives Memorial Piano: The Charles Ives Memorial Piano was donated by Ives's fellow members of the class of 1891, and apparently it has not been tuned since. As a result, it has the curious virtue of making any piece you play on it sound as if it were written by Charles Ives.

"Miles," said Nina, maddeningly calm, "you saw how the police were the other day. If we give this to them, they'll lock it in an evidence locker and forget about it. Besides, whatever is in that book, Professor Quinlan wanted to keep it a secret. That's why he took the book from you without letting you know why he really wanted it."

"Wait," I said. "You mean . . . he didn't actually love my paper?"

I supposed it made more sense. Still, it stung.

She stepped closer to me and lowered her voice. "Whatever the secret of the book is, I'm not letting *this* guy take it!" she said, crushing the email printout in her fist. "It's up to you and me, Miles."

I wanted to say, "Shouldn't Paul be helping you with this sort of thing?" But this time I managed to keep my mouth shut. Truth be told, I *did* kind of want to know the secret. Also, I kind of liked the sound of "you and me," when she said it.

"All right," I heard myself say. "We'll look at the book. But for the record, I was against this from the beginning."

"You're a prince among men, Miles," she said, flashing me that smile. She circled to the back of the folding chair and looked over my shoulder as I took *The Philogelos* out of my backpack.

"I really think this is all a mistake. I've read this whole book. Well, almost the whole book." I'd actually stopped three-quarters of the way through, pretty sure I would kill myself if I read another eunuch joke. I opened it cautiously. "Anyway, it's just a regular old what the . . . ?"

The inside of the front cover was ripped up. It looked like someone had sliced down the middle with a straight razor and then peeled back an inner layer of paper.

"I don't want to even guess what the fine is for this," I moaned.

"It wasn't like that before?" Nina said eagerly. "What about this?"

She bent over and gently picked up a yellowed slip of paper that had fluttered out of the pages when I'd opened the book. It hadn't been there yesterday. The piece of paper, I noticed, seemed about the right size to have come from inside the front cover.

She walked over to the piano and put it on the keys to stare down at it. "You're a humanities major, aren't you? This should be right up your alley." She patted the bench next to her. I walked over to her, and we both considered the paper silently.

It was a poem, which had been written with a fountain pen back in a time when handwriting really mattered:

Hayle jesterre! Thou hold'st in leather bounde
A humble joke-booke, held by most in ire
Renouncèd by scholars drap'd inne cap and gown
Keye to a hunte whych leadeth to gemme-stone fyre
No-one but thou alone now knowwe thys booke
Embodies treasure royaltie woulde eye
So reade the clew, decipher where to looke
Succeede, the Eli Opal waiting lies.

"Sounds like a **secret society** thing if you ask me," I said.

"What I don't get," mused Nina, "is if the professor knew this was hidden under the cover, how come he never bothered to check the book out himself?"

"It was misshelved," I told her. "I'm probably the first one to see it in decades."

I read the poem again. "So, any ideas?" I asked.

"Well, the first letters of each line spell out *Harkness*, obviously."

"Uh, yeah . . . obviously."

"That at least explains why the professor was up there."

"But it doesn't explain how he knew about this book in the first place. Or who killed him. Or what the hell the Eli . . ."

"It's a double acrostic!" she suddenly yelled. "Look at the first letter of the last word of every line."

I did this.

"What's a 'bigfbell'?"

"No! 'Big F bell!' It's telling us where in the tower to look!" She hit an F on the piano and then played a triumphant chord. "Ta da!"

"Impressive!" I said, casting a nervous glance at the crumpled printout of the threatening email. "So how do we get up the tower?"

secret society: Secret societies are one of Yale's most infamous traditions. Every year a new group of seniors is "tapped" for each of the twelve or so groups. The most prestigious have their own windowless stone buildings, known as "Tombs." The societies meet Thursday and Sunday nights, but almost nothing is known about what they do. (Maybe they watch *Family Guy*?) The general student consensus is that society membership is more a social thing than a vast conspiracy to take over the country . . . or is it?

> **Carillonneur:** The Guild of Carillonneurs is a competitive group to join, and its members are passionate enough about what they do to take regular trips around the world to check out other carillons. In 2006, they hosted the 64th Guild of Carillonneurs in North America Congress, which we gather is a big deal.
>
> **Harmony Place:** Harmony Place, run entirely by Yale students, provides a safe space for the homeless to watch movies, do laundry, socialize, or just get out of the cold.

"I have a . . . friend who's a **Carillonneur**," she said. "I'll borrow the keys from him and meet you there after dinner."

To my dismay, I remembered that Paul was a carillonneur.

"Who's this friend?" I asked innocently. "Do you think he'd want to come too?"

"Just this guy," she said quickly. "And I'd really rather not bring him into this. He couldn't come anyway. On Wednesdays he volunteers at **Harmony Place**."

"Sounds like a great guy," I mumbled.

CHAPTER
Six

Nina was there, waiting for me after dinner. She had changed into yoga clothes—soft rose-colored pants with a little lotus flower right on the base of the spine and a snowy white hoodie. She was delicate and perfect, with her red hair tucked behind her ears and her brown eyes fiercely determined. And she was Paul's, I reminded myself. I looked down at the wrinkled clothes I was still wearing and detected a faintly pizzalike smell coming from my shoulder. That couldn't be good. No. Nina was not for guys like me—guys who skimmed their reading, played only one instrument (and then, not well), wore red sneakers and old coats, and had shoulders that smelled like food.

A locked entrance to the right of the forbidden Branford Gate brought us into the base of the tower. Nina led the way up a narrow spiral staircase, and we came to an iron door that she used a different key on. Another spiral staircase led us through a room with the practice carillon and through another with, oddly enough, a **water tank**.

water tank: It's rumored that the water tank is used in carillonneur initiations. For what, we cannot say.

bells: Fifty-four bells, ranging four and a half octaves. It's the eighth largest carillon in North America.

East Rock: A 359-foot hill, with a neat-looking war monument on top. It's nine miles from Old Campus to the summit and back, and the view's more than worth it.

Center Church: New Haven's first church. Because it was built on top of the city's original burial ground, its crypt is one of the best-preserved colonial cemeteries in the United States. You can arrange a tour . . . if you dare!

Suddenly, the staircase opened into a space sixty feet tall, filled with forty-three tons of **bells**. There was no glass in the tall gothic windows, just wire mesh to keep out the pigeons, so the wind whipped through hard enough to make me sway. In front of us was a wooden frame six feet long, like a piano with levers instead of keys, and a row of pedals on the floor. Metal rods connected the console to the clappers in the bells suspended above.

I looked out at the New Haven skyline through the four green-tarnished copper clock faces. The view was breathtaking, with **East Rock** stained pink by the sunset. To the south was **Center Church**, with Sports Haven rearing incongruously beyond the highway.

"I always love the view from up here," said Nina.

"Oh, you've been up here before?" I asked, with studied nonchalance.

"Um, yeah, my friend took me up here a couple times."

"Look, Nina," I said, sighing. "You don't have to hide anything. I know you're dating Paul."

"Oh, okay." She didn't seem inclined to say anything more.

I took a deep breath and continued. "I guess the question is why you told me that the carillonneur you know is just *some guy*."

"I just thought he should be the one to tell you, since he's your friend and all," she said quickly.

"Oh, I guess that makes sense. It might have been a little awkward if you'd just said, 'Hey, I'm dating your old roommate.'"

"Exactly," she said, sounding relieved. "I just wanted to avoid the awkwardness."

Mission accomplished, I thought.

She led the way up another spiral staircase in the failing light. I was beginning to hate spirals. The wind got more intense, and my hand grew numb from clutching the ice-cold railing. My aching leg muscles made me wish that I'd managed to keep my resolution to go to the **gym** more than once a semester.

Each of the giant bells was embossed with the words "**For God, for Country, and for Yale!**," and, thankfully, the note they sounded. The largest F bell had what we were looking for. But it wasn't what we expected to find. There was no gem. Instead, there was another clue, etched inside the rim:

A CITY

SILVER

I wondered if the professor had killed himself after all, out of annoyance at these clues. I glanced above us. Twenty feet higher, the top of the staircase was cordoned off with yellow police tape.

gym: Each residential college has its own weight room, but when students say "go to the gym," they mean the Adrian C. "Ace" Israel Fitness Center at Payne Whitney, which has everything you'll need to wage war on the freshman fifteen.

For God, for Country, and for Yale!: The school's quasi-official motto. Yale may come third, but it's closest to the exclamation point.

New Haven: Students still have a lot of fun cracking jokes about how gritty New Haven is. New Haven used to be run-down (In 1998, *Money* magazine ranked New Haven the third most dangerous mid-size city in America). But Yale has spent a ton on security, and the city's been roaring back to life with boutiques and restaurants opening in neighborhoods that were boarded-up storefronts a decade ago. There was an increase in violent crime in 2005, but the large majority of students never feel like they're in danger. It's not perfectly safe, but it's no more dangerous than any other urban campus.

The other argument against New Haven is that, safety aside, it's a cultural wasteland. In fact, New Haven has more culture than most cities of its size. There are award-winning regional theaters, some of the best restaurants in the country, and everything's within walking distance to the campus. New Haven can't hold up to a metropolis like New York or Boston, but here's something to keep in mind: really big cities tend to overwhelm the campus. Ask a Columbia or NYU student how much they identify with their school. There aren't as many parties, events, or plain old watching movies and playing RISK, because the students spend their spare time exploring New York instead. And that's kind of a shame. There'll be plenty of time to enjoy a city when you're in your 20s—you only go to college once.

"Looks like Quinlan walked right past it," I said. What was he doing way up there? And who was he with?

"Do these clues seem just a little . . ." Nina started, "I don't know . . . silly? Like, Dan Brownish?"

It was true. Whoever put this here was of a different era. Yalies took their silly traditions more seriously in the old days, before the school went coed.

"So," she said, squinting at it. "Any ideas?"

"Well," I proposed halfheartedly, "the acrostic for this one is *as*."

She chuckled. "The Opal is hidden in a preposition?"

"Or maybe it's math," I suggested hopefully. "A city divided by silver equals a poor city. Which narrows it down to all of **New Haven**."

She curled her lip in concentration. It was a cute lip. "I think it's a rebus. You know, those visual-thinking puzzles?"

"Uh, no."

"You have the word *eggs* over the word *easy*," she explained, "and the answer is 'eggs over easy.'"

"A city over silver?" I said skeptically. She shrugged.

CHAPTER SIX

"Silver," I mused, stamping my feet against the cold. "Bullion . . . silver dollars . . .William Jennings Bryant . . ."

"Pounds sterling . . ." Nina suggested.

"A city above Sterling," I said, excitedly.

She looked at me inquisitively. "What does that mean?"

"Well, you've heard the rumor, right?" I said. "That there's a miniature Old Campus on top of **Sterling Library**."

"Really?" she said, with a wide-eyed freshman look. She started to head down, pushing past me on the narrow staircase. "Okay, the **stacks** don't close until eleven forty-five, so that gives us—"

"Wait a sec," I said, carefully hurrying after her. "We're not allowed to go up there!"

"So? We're not allowed to go up *here*, either."

My annoyance overcame my infatuation. "Hold it," I told her firmly. She stopped and looked over her shoulder impatiently. "Let's try and do this my way."

"Which is . . . ?" she asked skeptically.

Sterling Library: The legend is that too much stone was imported during construction, so the craftsmen used the extra materials to show off. An alternate rumor is that there's a whole stone city up there, complete with a stone golf course. Yet a third is that it's designed to hide the intake ducts for Sterling's massive climate control system.

stacks: The part of Sterling with the actual books, the stacks sprawl over seven floors (with each floor having two levels just to confuse you).

"We've got no proof that this Eli Opal even exists. Or that it wasn't found long ago. Let's do our research before we take any more risks."

"Fine. You can do your research if you want. Not my style. I'm going up there, with or without you."

"You won't be able to get up there," I warned her.

"So long, sucker! Don't come crying to me when I'm a billionaire!" She stuck her tongue out at me impishly and headed down the stairs, taking them two at a time.

"That's if the thing really exists!" I called after her. "Besides, I'm telling you, you won't get up there!"

"Nice try, but I know you're just trying to talk me out of it!"

Actually, I wasn't. Gary had told me that the door to the roof of Sterling had a padlock the size of a Hot Pocket. But I wasn't ready to worry about that yet. I had someone to see first.

Yale Unveiled

Cool Places at Yale You Probably Won't Be Allowed to Go

Like Miles, you too will be forbidden to see many of Yale's more interesting nooks! We are certainly not trying to get you to break any rules, but here are a whole bunch of them.

Social Robotics Lab
Dedicated to designing a robot named "Nico" that can socialize at the level of a nine-month-old baby. The lab also studies interactions between autistic children and cyborgs. Who can go there: mechanical engineering students.

Polo Room at Payne Whitney
There is a room with a wooden horse and a tilted floor, which one supposes is pretty much what polo is like. Award-winning gay erotica author Lawrence Schimel (class of '93) wrote a story about having sex on this. Who can go there: polo players.

The Vault at the Elizabethan Club
While it's neither secret nor threatening, the Elizabethan Club actually has more money than any secret society, including Skull and Bones. This is most flagrantly displayed in their absurd collection or rare books. The vault is opened every Friday afternoon, releasing literary treasures including a first edition of *Paradise Lost* and one of only three known copies of the 1604 *Hamlet*. Who can go there: members of the Lizzie and their guests.

Capuchin Cognition Lab

This is where they teach monkeys to use money, in the form of tokens. The lab became briefly famous when the *New York Times* reported that one of the monkeys had engaged in prostitution, something that the Capuchin keepers deny. Who can go there: graduate students, lab assistants, and monkeys.

The Steam Tunnels

As is common at large institutional complexes, an underground network of maintenance tunnels connects most of Yale's buildings. These supply the various structures with electricity, water, and heat, and it is the last that provides them with their colorful name. The steam tunnels are absolutely out of bounds for students, and very dangerous to wander around in. But people still do it sometimes and probably for those very reasons. It is rumored that students caught down there are immediately expelled. But those who have dared return with fabulous tales of bomb shelters full of rotting food. Who can go there: custodial staff and giant flesh-eating rats.

Yale University Wright Nuclear Structure Laboratory

Home of world's most powerful standalone tandem Van de Graaff accelerator. Students in Physics 206 will get to use a smaller Van de Graaff generator, which was used by the navy to irradiate food in the 1970s. Not as cool. Who can go there: NEEEEEEEEERDS!

Collection of Musical Instruments

Rare instruments from the 1500s to the present. Especially worth seeing: the Russian military bassoon, which looks like the bastard offspring of a bassoon, a trombone, and a Viking longship. Who can go there: well, everyone actually. But you'll be hard pressed to find a time to visit during the nine hours a week that it's open.

CHAPTER
Seven

Before I went to the tower that evening, I had Googled "Eli Opal," with no luck. Asking Gary about it was out of the question—he'd be so excited about a Yale treasure hunt that he'd probably kill me himself just to get the clue. But there was someone else who might be able to help.

I pushed my way though a crowd of people waiting for their lattes and entered the back half of "Koffee Too?" The tables were ruled by grad students, who arrived at nine in the morning to set up shop with their **course packets** and laptops and didn't leave until the place closed. They could be a territorial bunch, and I felt decidedly unwelcome as I peered at a dozen pairs of horn-rimmed glasses, trying to find a face I knew by reputation only.

I'd heard about her from Gary, of course. It had been during **Secret Society**

course packets: Course packets are thick—sometimes phonebook-thick—spiral-bound stacks of photocopied materials that professors make you buy. At the end of the class you have the choice of setting it on fire or keeping it around for years on the pretext that someday you'll read that one article you skipped, and then setting it on fire in 2018.

Secret Society Tap Night: In April, the societies come out from behind closed doors for one night only to initiate next year's members. This is done via bizarre public rituals that seem designed to make people curious.

> **Lawrance Hall:**
> Home of Stiles frosh, features three party suites: the Vault, the Jungle, and most notably the Lair. Lawrance connects to Phelps Hall, which means you can walk down the hall in your pj's and find a quiet classroom to read (or make out).
>
> **section:** Lecture classes usually require that you meet once a week in smaller groups led by a teaching assistant. You probably won't learn much in section, but participation is vital because the TA will usually grade your assignments. Make sure you do enough of the week's reading (five or ten pages) to make one or two intelligent comments per session—but talk too much and the rest of the class will hate you.

Tap Night. We were perched on my window seat in **Lawrance Hall**, watching ten people dressed as clowns run a relay race.

"Hey, that guy's in my **section**!" I had said. "What society do you think that is?"

"Scroll and Key," he said quickly.

"How the hell do you know that?"

He looked evasive for a minute.

"Spill," I demanded.

Gary looked around, which was ridiculous, because no one else was in the room. "Can you keep a secret?" he asked.

I smiled and raised a hand. "Scout's honor."

His voice dropped to a reverent whisper. "They call her the Post-Doc. Her real name's Ellery Mencil, but no one calls her that. She was an undergrad in linguistics, stayed to get a master's from the Div School, transferred to the Engineering School for a doctorate in fluid dynamics, then enrolled at the School of Arts and Sciences . . ." Gary trailed off, distracted, as a conga line of robed figures passed below our window, drunkenly singing "Rubber Ducky."

"And what does this have to do with Scroll and Key wearing clown suits?" I asked.

"A person learns a lot as a Yale student," Gary said proudly, as if he'd had something to do with it. "And she's been a Yale student longer than anyone else, ever. So she *knows things*. Everything. From what secret societies have planned for Tap Night, to what the dining hall is going to serve a year from next Wednesday."

"Wait, they plan that out ahead?"

Gary ignored me.

"The amazing thing is," he went on in a conspiratorial tone, "she somehow learns it all without ever leaving Koffee Too?!"

"Sure, and she was raised by wolves on East Rock, right?" I said, laughing.

Gary looked around nervously. "Not so loud," he whispered. "You never know what might get back to her!"

"So?"

"So if she likes you, your TA gives all your **problem sets** As! If she doesn't, all your sections will be scheduled for Friday mornings!" Gary's eyes were shining.

"Come on, she's just a grad student! If **GESO** has taught us anything, it's that grad students don't have any real power."

"Didn't you ever wonder how I got into **Gaddis** as a freshman?" Gary asked smugly.

"Wow," I said, genuinely impressed. "But how did you get her to help *you*?"

"There are rules, Miles," he had said solemnly. "There are procedures . . ."

I had been taught these rules and procedures, and I was about to put them into use.

I snapped out of my reverie as I finally spotted her sitting all alone in the back of the coffee shop,

problem sets: The equivalent of papers for the math and science crowd. People tend to do these in groups, which makes them go a lot faster. Be warned—some professors have no conception of what constitutes an "easy," or even "solvable," question for undergrads.

GESO: The Graduate Employees and Students Organization is a group of grad students who want to unionize and have the university treat them like employees. They've been unsuccessful for many years, which most undergrads feel okay about, since anything that makes their TAs unhappy can only be good.

Gaddis: The Cold War, one of the most popular courses at Yale, is taught by the world's foremost expert on the subject. Much of the course is spent watching a CNN miniseries on the Cold War that the professor consulted on. Still, getting into this as a freshman is essentially impossible.

her books and papers covering every square inch of the tabletop. She was just as the Puh had described her: her hair as dark as photocopier ink, her skin as white as notepaper. I approached her nervously.

Ten feet from her table, a large man with a larger beard rose from his seat and blocked my path. "State your business," he growled.

"I want to talk to Ellery," I said. Behind him, she was leafing through a book, highlighter in hand. I couldn't guess her age—never seeing the sun can do wonders for your skin.

"The Post-Doc is writing a paper," he said, crossing his arms.

"I have something for her," I said, holding up a $6 edition of Aeschylus that I'd purchased at Labyrinth Books, as per the instructions. I ruffled the pages under my thumb, and the Post-Doc glanced up at the sound.

The bearded man looked at her. She nodded and he stepped aside.

I gingerly pulled out the chair across from her and placed the book in the center of the table. She continued reading without looking at me.

"Who is that guy?" I asked her.

"**Forestry** student," she said into her book. "They make good muscle." She talked like it wasn't worth her time to open her mouth all the way.

"Miss Mencil," I began, "I'm—"

"Miles Bowman," she interrupted. "Sophomore, Ezra Stiles, humanities major. Recently met with

---

Forestry: The Forestry School is one of Yale's more interesting graduate programs. The students spend a lot of time off campus, roaming around the 10,880 acres of New England woods that Yale has purchased and set aside as their private classroom. At commencement, the forestry students decorate their mortarboards with shrubbery.

Dean Sheely, concerning the death of Professor Quinlan. And I see you've recently gotten a haircut. It looked better longer. It's too curly to keep it that short."

I reached up and nervously ran my hand over my recently trimmed hair.

"What else do you know about me?" I asked in wonder.

She highlighted a sentence in her book. "Self-knowledge is a worthy pursuit, but that's not why you came to see me, is it?"

"Have you heard of the Eli Opal?" I asked.

She slammed her book shut abruptly, picked up the Aeschylus I'd brought her, and sniffed the binding. "You support local business, I see," she said approvingly.

"Nothing but," I lied. Gary had told me about this, too. Someone had once given her a gift certificate for the Gap, and he'd flunked out by the end of the semester.

She arched an eyebrow at me thoughtfully, but replaced the book on the table without comment. "Jeremiah Quinlan was your favorite professor, wasn't he?"

"Sure, but—"

"Why have you not read his work?"

"I have! **Both his books**," I protested.

She gave me a sardonic hint of a smile. "Not the books, Miles."

Both his books: A lot of Yale professors have made their reputations by publishing extensively, and reading your professor's work can be a lot of fun. It's like Googling your new significant other.

As if this had reminded her, she flipped her own book open and returned to her reading.

"Hold on," I said, "what do you mean, 'not the books'?" She didn't answer, but I heard a chair push back from a table and looked over to see the forestry student standing and fingering the Leatherman tool on his belt. I took one last look at the Post-Doc's inscrutable face and made my way toward the exit. When I looked back, the Aeschylus had vanished.

Drink Up!
New Haven Coffee Shops

Whether you're looking for a quick jolt of caffeine, a comfortable study spot, or that ineffably pretentious coffee shop atmosphere, New Haven's got you covered. The stores listed below are only a small selection.

Barnes & Noble Campus Bookstore Cafe

Nestled all the way in the back of the second floor of the bookstore, this coffee shop is nice because it's right next to the ginormous magazine rack. (Technically, you're not supposed to read them without buying, but they won't hassle you as long as you don't spill your mocha all over the pictures.) Plus, you can find pretty much anything you need to buy under the same roof. For starters, they have a gargantuan selection of books that *aren't* textbooks, but that's not all. We can't tell you how many times we've found ourselves saying, "You know what would go great with this coffee? A package of lightbulbs! And a beanbag chair! And a giant beer stein with a Yale logo printed on it!" Okay, so we've never said that. Still, the campus bookstore has all these things, which is somehow comforting.

What to order: a banana and cream frappucino. Goes down nicely while you're sweating over your Orgo textbook.

Starbucks

In some places, Starbucks is the most pretentious coffee option available. New Haven is not one of these places. The only pretentious people at the New Haven Starbucks are the ones who claim not to care about being called Yuppie Scum.

What to order: anything Venti.

Café Atticus

A bookstore/café that gains pretension points for it's location beneath the British Art Center, and for offering fresh baked bread daily. But the inevitable gaggle of poor students who congregate outside at midnight to the get the free, stale, leftover bread takes it back down to unpretentious.

What to order: free, stale, leftover bread, natch (although their tiramisu is unsurpassed).

Willoughby's

Willoughby's is a good place to go if you have a tattoo, or a piercing, or if you can deliver an impromptu lecture on the importance of supporting sustainable shade-grown free-trade coffee as opposed to the regular cash-crop variety. If you have the lecture tattooed on your buttocks, so much the better. If you let it slip that you've ever been inside a Starbucks, the regulars will probably swarm and stone you to death. So pretentious that it comes out the other side.

What to order: the immediate overthrow of the capitalist state.

Koffee?

You'll find the original Koffee? way down Whitney Avenue. It makes up for being in the boondocks by offering plenty of comfy couches and free wireless internet access. The only thing pretentious here is the spelling—but that's pretty pretentious.

What to order: the "Viennese Coffee," also known as "a big warm cup of half & half with just enough coffee to make it light brown" or "a heart attack waiting to happen."

Koffee Too?

Centrally located, the sheer amount of traffic coming through here makes it the Grand Central Station of coffee shops. Grad students will get here at nine in the morning to find a table and set up shop with a stack of books and a laptop until they're forcibly ejected at the end of the night. So you're not likely to find a seat, much less get any reading done. Pretentiousness? High. Some of the grad students positively radiate the stuff, plus the silly name factor of Koffee Too?'s sister store is essentially doubled here. We have no idea why there's a question mark in the name.

What to order: a double espresso, on your way to your next two-hour-long lecture.

Book Trader

A used bookstore/coffee shop, its shelves are fun to browse while you're waiting for adorably named sandwiches like "Call Me Fish'mael." There's a nice outdoor area for the warmer weather.

What to order: chai tea. In fact, all anyone seems to order here is chai tea—not coffee, not vaguely literary sandwiches, and certainly not books. It's a wonder that the place stays in business, but it seems to be going strong.

MoKa

Technically, a hot chocolate store. But they sell coffee too, making it no different than any of the many coffee shops that sell hot chocolate. As you might guess from the name, this is another spin-off from the java barons at Koffee?, who can have a veritable empire in the New Haven area.

What to order: not hot chocolate. Don't give them the satisfaction.

CHAPTER
Eight

I headed for the **music library** in Sterling, which was my favorite place to do research. Sitting at one of the workstations, I plugged "Jeremiah Quinlan" into every humanities database I could think of. It was strange to realize that he was someone whose ideas were studied in classrooms around the country. Articles he'd published popped up everywhere, and I skimmed them tentatively, unsure of what I was looking for. It was hard to find a common thread to his writings—literature, of course, but also the history of science and even a monograph on eighteenth-century bookbinding.

And then there it was: a 1986 essay in the now-defunct journal *Myth* called "The Mystery of the Eli Opal."

I looked at my watch. Theoretically, I had a section to be at. But my TA had some sort of undecipherable accent, and besides, I'd been

music library: The music library used to be a courtyard—the walls are still weather-beaten brick, capped with a vaulted art-deco ceiling. People like to come here to study because it's got natural light and the comfortable chairs. But with all the comfortable open space, the designers didn't leave much room for books, which are mostly cramped in an overheated basement.

CHAPTER EIGHT | 58

Shopping Period: The two weeks between when classes begin and when schedules must be finalized. Yalies are free to walk in and out of classes at will, idly browsing the department store windows of Knowledge. This is not to say that you're automatically in whatever class you show up for. If it's overcrowded, the professor will probably begin the second or third meeting by kicking out underclassmen, or nonmajors. But the beauty of Shopping Period is that there are dozens of other classes just waiting for you to walk through the door.

Starr Main Reference Room: A huge room with 55,000 reference volumes and students who will shush you if you so much as blink.

Elihu Yale: To get the university named after him, Elihu donated 417 books, a portrait of King George, and three "bales of goods." If you donated that much nowadays, they might name a water fountain after you.

gradually losing interest in the class since **Shopping Period**.

So instead I found the appropriate volume in the **Starr Main Reference Room** and brought it back to the music library so I could read it in a comfy chair. The article answered some questions. It raised a whole lot more.

In 1802, Quinlan wrote, a young lawyer named Benjamin Silliman was appointed Yale's first natural history professor. Being completely ignorant of the sciences, Silliman's first act was to take the university's entire collection of minerals and gemstones to Philadelphia, to study with the great naturalist James Woodhouse.

While there, Silliman catalogued one particularly exciting item: an enormous opal with a vivid blue coloring unheard of in a specimen of that size. Reports varied on its origins—one source said it was part of **Elihu Yale**'s original contribution to the university. Woodhouse was quick to declare it the most valuable opal in the New World.

In 1804, Silliman packed the specimens up and headed for Connecticut. But when he returned the stones to their cases in New Haven, the Opal was not among them. He issued a formal apology to the president of the college, in which he expressed complete bafflement as to its disappearance. An inquiry was held, and the gem was declared "accidentally misplaced." Silliman went to his grave still expressing regret at losing such a treasure.

The gem was never returned, nor was there any report of it being offered for sale, legally or otherwise. For many decades afterward, the story of the Opal was a popular campus tale. Indeed, it grew in the telling—later accounts are full of intrigue, deception, and ghosts. One popular version even hinted that the Opal had been stolen by members of **Skull and Bones**. Eventually, most Yalies assumed that the gem was a mere legend. But Silliman's correspondence survives, and his precise observations on the size and quality of the Opal suggest that were it around today, it would be among the world's most priceless jewels. The tale declined in popularity in the early nineteenth century, and today only the oldest Yale alumni still smile at the mention of the fabled "Eli Opal."

Professor Quinlan ended the article on a personal note: "The tragedy of the Opal is that it was enjoyed only by those who stole it, when it should have been the marvel of millions, and now it may be forever lost. Were it in its rightful place in the **Peabody Museum**, it would surely be, as Silliman once wrote, 'A radiant example of the majesty of God, as reflected in the beauty of the natural world.'"

I set aside the volume and stared up at the high, arched ceiling. So the professor had known exactly what the Eli Opal was. But he'd known things that he'd kept out of the article. For instance, he'd known that a lost jokebook was the key to finding it. And he said in the article that the gem had been

Skull and Bones: The most famous of the secret societies, thanks to its many alumni who have gone on to positions of power. (For instance, both George W. Bush and John Kerry were members.) It was the inspiration for the Joshua Jackson movie *The Skulls*, which is regularly screened on campus to hilarious laughter. The Bones tomb is a windowless building of brown sandstone on High Street. Freshmen will dare each other to run up and knock on the door like it's Boo Radley's house.

Peabody Museum: This natural history museum operated by the university is famous for its extensive collection of dinosaurs. Free to members of the Yale community, and it's a good place to take your parents when they visit.

stolen, even though the university had declared it only "misplaced."

After I'd left his office yesterday, Quinlan had clearly read the clue, figured it out, and gone to Harkness to find the Opal, presumably intending to give it to the Peabody. But it seemed that someone hadn't wanted that to happen. Someone who had known about the clue almost as soon as Quinlan had, and had been willing to kill to stop him. Someone who had then threatened Nina to get the clue for himself.

However, my nervousness was matched by a growing sense of excitement. The most valuable opal in the New World. With that, I could kiss my **student loans** goodbye. I headed back to the workstation and did a little research on selling gems. "Miles Bowman, millionaire playboy." Sounded good, maybe even better than the Betts Prize thing.

I was already planning the shape of my pool when my phone vibrated. It was Nina.

"So," she said, "do any interesting research?"

"A bit. You were right about the Opal being real," I admitted.

"Yeah, well you were right about me not being able to get up to the top of Sterling. Any ideas?"

"Well," I said. "Actually, I *do* have one . . ."

---

student loans: Around 40 percent of Yalies receive some sort of financial aid, which has become more plentiful in recent years thanks to competition among the Ivies.

Shop Till You Drop
Shopping Period Strategies

Miles wouldn't be the first Yale sophomore to drink too deep of the heady liquor of Shopping Period and wind up with a boring class. Here are some of the ways that Yalies cope with this amazing—but intimidating—tradition.

The Explorer
This person is determined to visit every single class Yale has to offer. He has a spreadsheet with forty courses plugged into it and visits twelve a day. He often leaves courses he loves midway to visit part of another one. The thing is, anyone this organized probably secretly has his whole schedule pretty much figured out, but he still feels compelled to attend as many classes as he possibly can, just to make sure he doesn't miss anything.

Siesta King
He won't go to a single course until the last couple days of Shopping Period. It's not that this person is lazy—he'll work incredibly hard once the semester gets going. But it's for this very reason that he can't bear to let go of vacation quite yet. Instead, he spends a few days sleeping and moping before picking all his classes at the last minute in a flurry of soul-searching and dart throwing. Most classes do cover material during Shopping Period, so the Siesta King starts the semester already one week behind. Presumably this fulfills some deep-seated psychological need.

Seminar Connoisseur

The more difficult the course is to get into, the more this guy has his heart set on it. Senior-only seminars, residential college seminars, even grad school courses—he was just born to take them. He'll spend Shopping Period writing essays to big-name professors and rushing to department offices first thing in the morning to see if the list of students has been posted yet. Spends the rest of the year boasting to his friends about how amazing his ultra-exclusive class is, while secretly wondering why it feels like any other class.

The Tourist

Whereas the Explorer is hacking through the jungle, searching for the El Dorado of perfect courses, the tourist is strolling around Madrid with a camera before flying back to her apartment in Hoboken. She has her classes picked but out of sheer curiosity shops classes she has no intention of taking. Hieroglyphics. Film Noir. Intro to Sculpture. To the Tourist, Shopping Period is vacation from her major. If she picks up a syllabus, it's just for the scrapbook.

The Waffler

The Waffler fears Shopping Period like a jailbird fears his first whiff of freedom. He will not only switch courses three times each day, he'll switch majors. He will beg his friends to tell him what the good courses are . . . and then waffle over them. The night before his schedule is due he'll be up weeping in the common room, agonizing over a pile of syllabi like it was Sophie's Choice. Inevitably, this person will hate all his classes. "Why, oh why did I take microeconomics! Macro! Macro, that was the way to go!"

The Belushi
"Why would I get up before noon, when there are three hundred courses that meet only in the afternoon? Why should I have class on Friday? Why should I have any final exams? Or any papers?" The Belushi only picks classes that accommodate his busy schedule of beer pong. After two years of taking whatever random courses meet on Tuesday and Thursday afternoons, he'll probably wake up one day and realize that without meaning to, he's become a Medieval Studies major. And serve him right! But the Belushi isn't one to wallow in angst—he'll probably just let his beard grow out and acquire a taste for mead.

The North Star
She picks her five courses over vacation and sticks with them. She'll be done with her first papers by the time most people pick up their syllabi. One is more likely to acquire this stability junior and senior years, partially because you have more required courses to complete your major, partially because you realize that you'll probably enjoy whatever classes you choose. But if you do it your freshman year, you're one of two things: a premed, or incurably dull.

CHAPTER
Nine

I leaned against a pillar in the main hall of Sterling while Nina finished reading a photocopy of the professor's article. She let out a long, low whistle.
"I can see why Quinlan was so excited," she said. "If we find this thing, we'll be on the cover of . . . well, whatever a major archeological journal is, we'll be on the cover of it."

"I feel bad about not telling Gary what's really going on," I said.

"I know I was nonchalant earlier about the whole threatening email," she said nervously, "but are you sure we had to get your friend involved with this?"

"Gary's the only person I know who's actually been on the roof," I explained. "He's in **YSECS**." Actually, he'd been trying to get me to go up there with him for months now, promising that it was the coolest place in the world. I always told him it wasn't worth getting ExCommed for.

"So what did you tell him?"

YSECS: The Yale Society for the Exploration of Campus Secrets. Often referred to by its acronym (because it sounds like "Y-Sex"). A semi-secret group dedicated to finding the many hidden rooms, dead-end hallways, and other architectural anomalies that are scattered about the campus.

> **improv:** Yale has a thriving improv comedy scene. The Viola Question (the best of the groups) holds a twelve-hour improv marathon on Cross Campus every spring, the last thirty minutes of which are definitely worth showing up for.

I looked at my sneakers. "Um. I told him there's this incredibly hot girl I'm trying to impress."

She guffawed. "Me? Hot? You should be in an **improv** group. Still, that's pretty smooth thinking."

There's nothing more attractive than a pretty girl who doesn't realize she's pretty, I thought, trying not to blush.

"I just hope he doesn't attract any attention," she said, worried again. "That email was pretty definite about not getting anyone involved . . ."

"Don't worry," I said. "Gary takes this kind of thing seriously. I'm sure he won't . . ."

It was at that point that Gary arrived. He was wearing full military fatigues, tossing a pair of bolt cutters and grinning like an idiot.

"Sorry I'm late," he said. "You must be Nina. You ready to have your mind blown?"

Nina stared at him.

"We're all sooooooo murdered . . ." she said under her breath.

I snatched the bolt cutters and stuffed them in my backpack, next to *The Philogelos*.

"Gary," I said with a sigh, "did you have to wear camouflage face paint too? There's no way you're getting into the stacks like that."

Gary smiled and strode over to the security guard, who gave him a high five on his way to the elevator. We showed our IDs and hurried after him.

"I play 'capture the flag' here with the **Freestyle Dueling Association**," the Puh explained, hitting the button for floor Seven. "That guy would be surprised if I showed up not wearing camo."

The lock, though large, was no match for the cutters. I pushed the tiny door open with my shoulder, allowing the dismembered padlock to clatter to the floor. The three of us walked onto the rooftop. The Puh brushed away a tear. "It's so beautiful!" he gasped. "Every time I come up here I promise myself I won't cry."

In front of us was a shrunk-down **Old Campus**, about twenty feet wide. The buildings were barely taller than us but completely detailed, with stone gutters, tiny shingles, and windows etched in bas-relief. The door we'd entered from was right where the **High Street Gate** would have been, and we wandered into the mini-quad.

"If I ever have children," said the Puh, "this is where I want them to be born. No! *Conceived*." He didn't seem to be kidding.

"Amazing," I muttered, running my hand along a stone log fence. "Everything except the grass." I thought about how gorgeous the real Old Campus looked in the spring and felt a case of **sophomore slump** coming on.

I drifted over to the miniature version of the Woolsey statue and rubbed its foot for good luck—no one does this to the real statue, but I figured it couldn't hurt. The tiny stone foot cracked off. I

Freestyle Dueling Association: We all go through a phase where we think pretend sword fights are an awesome way to spend time. For most people this is the summer between third and fourth grade. For the FDA, it's every Sunday, from two to five, right out in public where everyone can watch. But it should be noted that, like many people engaged in "dorky" activity, FDA members seem to be having more fun than the people mocking them.

Old Campus: The authors have no evidence this exists, but like to believe it does.

High Street Gate: The gate across from Harkness Tower.

sophomore slump: As a freshman, the world revolves around you. You have a gaggle of different advisers to make sure you're happy, you can take classes without worrying about your major, and upperclassmen are trying to recruit you for every organization they belong to. As a sophomore, all of this goes away, and it can be a downer.

Phelps Gate: Phelps Gate is a broad, arching tunnel leading from College Street to the Old Campus. To generations of freshmen who arrived on campus dragging their suitcases across its cobblestones, Phelps is the unofficial entrance to the university: Yale's Ellis Island.

Freshman Screw: Screws are held by each college, plus there's a big one for the whole freshman class. Everybody is supposed to be set up by his or her roommate with a surprise date. This gives you an opportunity to either "screw" your roommate, or to get your roommate "screwed," depending on if you're feeling generous or vindictive.

Connecticut Hall: Connecticut Hall is the oldest building at Yale, dating from 1752. Noah Webster and Nathan Hale once slept there. Now it has offices for the Comp Lit and Philosophy departments, but more importantly, a 24-hour computer cluster.

sexile: To be "sexiled" is to be kicked out of a double so that your lucky roommate can get lucky.

long-distance: What's that? You really love your high school girlfriend? You share one soul? Too bad! You're dooooooomed! Seriously, these things last maybe a year until you both realize you've grown apart, and you're sick of keeping track of each other's friends you've never met.

looked at it mournfully and placed it in Woolsey's lap, hoping Gary hadn't noticed.

"I bet the view from here is awesome!" said Nina. She crawled through the mini–**Phelps Gate** to look around the outside. Gary and I strolled around the miniature quad, lost in our thoughts.

"Wow. That's the bench where I had to stand with my pants around my ankles for the **Freshman Screw**," said Gary.

"Guess I'm not going to be taking Nina to her Screw," I muttered, quietly enough so she wouldn't hear. "Paul will probably parachute in for the occasion or something." I sat on **Connecticut Hall**, and the Puh sat next to me. "At least I have a single now, and he can't **sexile** me like last year."

"Don't worry, Miles. I can't imagine a girl coming up here and not falling head over heels with the guy who brought her. But you don't have to worry about me, since I'm still doing the **long-distance** thing."

"How is Meredith, by the way?"

"Um . . . haven't talked to her for a little while, actually."

"Oh," I said. "Is something wrong?"

"So Nina," said the Puh loudly.

"Right, Nina. I dunno, I'm having second thoughts. Even if she was interested in me, Paul's a . . ." A what? Nemesis? Freak of nature? ". . . a friend. I wouldn't want to ruin their relationship."

"But if she really likes you, it's not like they had much of a relationship to ruin, right? Besides, maybe it'll turn out he's been cheating on her all along. Or that he's secretly **gay**."

"Not likely. He's too good to be cheating on her, and too well-adjusted to be hiding from his own sexuality."

"Hey Miles . . ." yelled Nina over the wall. "Can you come out here?"

Gary gave me a thumbs up as I crawled outside, shivering in the cold night wind.

Nina was looking at the entrance to mini-Phelps. "What does it say above the real Phelps Gate?"

"Not sure," **I admitted**.

"Well, look what it says here." She indicated the inscription.

"*Canis Id Devoravit*," I read. "I think it means 'The Dog Ate It.'"

"You read Latin?"

"Nah, just took some SAT prep."

"The dog . . . maybe that means **Handsome Dan**," she said. "But he's just a puppy! He couldn't possibly—"

gay: In the late eighties, the wife of a faculty member wrote an article in the *Wall Street Journal* accusing Yalies of rampant homosexuality. Although her estimate that a quarter of the student body was gay was (probably) not true, Yale gained a reputation as the "Gay Ivy," and the LGBT Co-op still likes to brag, "One in four, maybe more." Whatever the numbers, the most remarkable thing about being gay at Yale is how unremarkable it is. You and your boyfriend can walk through campus holding hands, and people will barely notice. A lot of the gay-rights organizations exist more as social clubs than as activist groups.

I admitted Actually, it says "Lux Et Veritas" ("Light and Truth"), Yale's official motto.

Handsome Dan: The current Handsome Dan is the sixteenth to bear that name. The original was the first live college mascot in America in 1889. See our guide to Handsome Dans on pages 97–98! All your Handsome Dan questions answered!

Payne Whitney Gymnasium: The largest building on the Yale campus. In fact, it's the largest gym in the country. Some people may think this is overcompensating; our football team doesn't make Sportscenter too often. In any case, the House of Payne has got everything from the only squash court in America with four glass walls, to indoor crew tanks, to the world's largest pool not on the ground floor, weighing a somewhat ludicrous 2.25 million pounds. Why they put it on the third floor, no one knows.

Women's Table: In 1993, Yale invited Vietnam War Memorial designer Maya Lin ('82) to design a monument to women at the university. She produced an oval of smooth granite, with the number of women studying at Yale each year from its founding to the present arranged in a spiral. In nice weather, a layer of water spills over its surface. Consequently, the Women's Table is routinely slid upon by naked, drunk frat boys.

"What about *the* Dan?" I asked. "They stuffed the first Handsome Dan. He's on display at the **Payne Whitney Gymnasium**."

"Ewwwww," she said.

I thought about it for a minute. "Yeah. Ewwwww."

"Enjoying the view?" yelled Gary.

"It's so romantic!" Nina shouted back. I could practically see him grinning, convinced I was well on my way to second base.

The view was pretty amazing. I took a couple of steps toward the edge of the roof to get a better look. After you're at Yale a while, you can lose your sense of awe—gargoyles and crenellations are just things that buildings have. The top of Sterling made me feel like a freshman again.

I looked over the edge again and frowned. Behind the **Women's Table**, I could just make out a figure wearing a dark coat and a black fedora. The figure seemed to be looking up. And I could almost swear there was light reflecting off a pair of binoculars.

Probably a bird watcher, I thought. Lots of birds on campus. Or squirrels. Nocturnal, library-dwelling squirrels. I shivered. Still, it was probably nothing. No sense in worrying Nina.

"Well, we better get out of here before the place closes," I said briskly, crawling back through Phelps.

"If we get locked in, everyone will assume that the three of us were having **sex**."

"Have a good time?" asked Gary.

"Oh yes!" said Nina, heading over to the exit. "It's the most beautiful place I've ever seen! Thank you, Miles, for bringing me up here!" She gave me a lingering, affectionate hug. She was an *atrocious* actress, but Gary only saw what he wanted to see. He gave me a wink. I felt bad for deceiving him, but given where the hunt was headed now, there was no question of telling him the truth.

It was midnight when I returned to my room. Gary had headed off, still in camo, to a merengue party at **La Casa Cultural**, and Nina had gone to do at least some of the reading for her **freshman seminar**.

The Stiles **SAC** had invited everyone to nachos, but I had a ten-page paper to write and eight hours in which to write it. I might have to pull an all-nighter, but tomorrow was Friday, and I'd have all of Thanksgiving break to catch up on sleep.

Of course, the first thing I did when I got home was check my email. I spent twenty minutes reading discuss-list posts debating the finer points of the great training montages of movie history before I noticed that my room had been ransacked.

In my defense, it wasn't the easiest thing to notice—the total amount of mess was roughly the same, just redistributed. Looking to see what could be missing, I immediately noticed a suspiciously

sex: Sex in the stacks is a Yale tradition, albeit one much more talked about than actually done.

La Casa Cultural: The Cultural Houses are run by Yale to provide a sense of community to minority students. They host lectures and events, but more importantly, they have pretty generous budgets to throw parties, which are open to the entire campus.

freshman seminar: Starting in 2004, Yale began offering small freshmen-only seminars, all taught by Yale's big-name professors.

SAC: Social Activities Committee. Every college has this group of students, who are given funds to do things like organizing bowling trips and decorating the common room.

> **Tyco Copy:** This is Yale's main destination for course packets. For some reason, they display a large picture of a kid in a baseball uniform from around 1981.

> **entryway:** Rather than laying out the rooms horizontally (by floors, like most dorms), Yale has "entryways." Each college courtyard has a dozen or so of these big old wooden doors leading into spiral staircases with suites on every floor. Get used to climbing stairs.

vacant patch of floor. That morning, it had contained a stack of library books. Now there was just a scrap of paper with a note:

"We have your books. To get them back, go to **Tyco Copy**, have them make a reproduction of the next clue, and hold it there for a Mr. Marlowe. We hope we don't need to tell you to forget that you ever heard of the Eli Opal."

My scream of anguish was probably heard in the next **entryway**. I needed those books for my paper.

Interestingly, although only that afternoon I'd considered giving *The Philogelos* to either the murderer or the police without a second thought, now cooperating didn't occur to me as an option. Maybe after risking expulsion to go after two clues, I was too caught up in the mystery and excitement of the thing. Maybe it was the kidney-shaped swimming pool I hoped to buy once I cashed the gem in. Or maybe I didn't want to let Nina down.

Unfortunately, nothing about the state of my room seemed to offer any clue as to the identity of my visitor. I found myself wishing I'd gone to last week's **Master's Tea** with the technical advisors from *CSI: Miami*. And there was no way to stake out Tyco Copy and see who picked up the package—the place got too much traffic. He or she was clever—I had to give him or her that.

Ruefully, I leaned back in my chair and considered my next step. If I gave up the clue, Snatchy McBookgrabber would start racing me to the Opal. On the other hand, if I didn't, I was a target, and maybe Nina too.

Then I had an idea.

Gritting my teeth, I wrote an email to the prof for my **residential college seminar** requesting an **extension** on the paper and got to work on fooling Snatchy.

At the ungodly hour of nine the next morning, I walked into Tyco. It had been a long night after all, dying paper with coffee and tracking down Perfect Paul to borrow his calligraphy set. (I had to promise to buy two tickets to his **jam**.) My handwriting lacked the fluidity of the original, but the results would do. I slapped the phony clue down on the counter.

Master's Tea: Recent invitees have included Steven King, Frank Oz, and Monica Lewinsky.

residential college seminar: Courses taught by experts from outside the university. They tend to be off the beaten track: The Comic Book as Literature and Forensic Entomology (that is, bugs in dead guys) are two prime examples. Demand is understandably high, so getting into a residential college seminar takes luck and determination. It helps if you're in the college that's sponsoring the class.

extension: When you just can't get something done, appealing to your professor directly is often a better bet than trying to get a Dean's Excuse. The phrase "I really want to feel like I'm submitting the best work I can" is usually good for at least an extra day. Professors don't want to read a rushed paper any more than you want to give them one.

jam: A capellese for "really long concert."

CHAPTER NINE | 74

Beinecke: The Beinecke Rare Book Library has not only invaluable first editions, but literally millions of maps and documents. People come from all over the world to do research here. Others come just to marvel at the architecture: the walls are thin slabs of translucent marble and from inside the library they seem to glow with the sunlight. Most of the building is empty space, with an immense glass cube of book stacks in the center. Only librarians are allowed in, for good reason— in the event of fire, the Beinecke stacks are flooded with argon gas, killing the fire along with anyone unlucky enough to be there at the time.

Gutenberg Bible: The first book ever printed with moveable type, the Gutenberg Bible is so expensive that even God probably can't afford it. Beinecke keeps its copy on display in a special case, and turns one page every day. So if illuminated marginalia is your thing, make sure to stop by occasionally.

The copy guy frowned at it:
Hayle ye seekere of yon Opale!
The nexte clew doth lie in ye **Beinecke**
Bound up in the spine of ye **Gutenberg Bible**.
Goode Lucke! Ye wille neede itte.

"Make five hundred copies of this," I told him. "Hold under the name Marlowe. He'll pay when he picks them up." I walked to the door and turned back. "Almost forgot. Make those color copies! And use the most expensive paper!"

Residential Colleges

Yale is made up of twelve residential colleges—this is where you live, eat, study, and play. Your residential college will determine much of your Yale identity. It's your team. Your people. You can't know too much about the colleges. Start now.

Incoming freshmen are randomly placed in one of the colleges, where they will live for most of their Yale careers, but the colleges are much more than dorms. Each has its own dining hall, library, snack bar (aka the "Buttery"), laundry, gym, and tutors. For many Yalies, their college is the center of their social life; Yale doesn't have a student center, and no one misses it. The college system is based on Oxford and Cambridge, not on Hogwarts, as is commonly believed.

Berkeley

Namesake: Right Reverend (later Bishop) George Berkeley (1685–1753), who endowed Yale with a gift of land and books

Mascot: the Thunder-Chicken (you heard us)

Pros: Berkeley's organic dining hall, with the menu designed by celebrity chef Alice Waters, is widely considered the best food on campus.

Cons: The fancy dining hall is only open to Berkeleyites and their guests, making Berkeley the Slytherin of Yale's residential colleges. (Not to encourage the Harry Potter/Hogwarts theme.)

Notable Architecture and Features

Straddling Cross Campus, Berkeley is really two mini-colleges. The tunnel connecting the two halves of Berkeley is covered in elaborate murals.

Events and Customs

Berkeley Bishop Bash: This event includes a medieval dinner (at which no utensils or plates are used) followed by a "dungeon party." What this has to do with Bishop Berkeley, who lived long after the Middle Ages, no one is sure.

Berkeley Streak: Berkeleyites strip down and charge across the Old Campus during Bulldog Days. Whether this is meant to encourage the pre-frosh to enroll or to stay away is an open question.

North Court vs. South Court snowball fight: The convenient thing about Berkeley's divided status is that they can be their own rival.

Branford

Namesake: The town of Branford, Connecticut, which briefly housed Yale before it moved to sunny New Haven

Mascot: the squirrel

Pros: Robert Frost once called its Great Courtyard "the loveliest courtyard in America." Plus, Branford contains the Yale landmark par excellence, Harkness Tower.

Cons: Frank Lloyd Wright once said that if he could be anywhere in the world, it would be "on top of Harkness Tower—so that I wouldn't have to *look* at it." Plus, living in Branford means you're closer to the carillon than anyone else at Yale, which is fun for about a week.

Notable Architecture and Features

The God Quad: A four-person suite with a big common room. Not as impressive as some of the other party suites, but more fun to say. And they do get official funds from the college for . . . soda. And chips.

Events and Customs

Branford Independence Day: For one day, Branford secedes from the rest of Yale but somehow always decides to return.

In addition to the notorious Branford Gate, there's a millstone in the center courtyard that carries a terrible curse. Apparently you're not supposed to step on it.

The Branford master is a diehard Yankees fan who brings his students on a yearly pilgrimage to the hallowed Bronx.

Calhoun

Namesake: John C. Calhoun (1782–1850), alumnus, statesman, and pro-slavery orator. As the official Calhoun website carefully states, "there is no direct connection between the college and the man, and he is neither founder nor patron." In other words, they'd really rather not change the name, since they already printed up the T-shirts.

Mascot: the hound

Pros: Claire Danes is a recent alumna.

Cons: The dining hall is widely considered the worst on campus. That and the slavery thing.

Notable Architecture and Features

There's a secret entrance to the residential college library from the common room—or at least there is if the right doors are propped open.

Bookworld: An immense two-story suite with a giant balcony known as the "Castle." It's called Bookworld because in the days of yore one of its inhabitants stole a big ol' sign that said "Bookworld" and hung it on the wall.

The basement contains a sauna (seldom working) and the Cabaret, a popular performance space. Conveniently, the Cabaret connects to the Buttery so you can get a side of mozzarella sticks with your slam poetry.

Events and Customs

The Trolley Party: Celebrates the day in 1949 when New Haven's trolley service was shut down. This may win the "lamest excuse for a party" award.

Houndfest: Another party, with a different theme each year. Recently, it was a Wild West theme party complete with mechanical bull.

Davenport

Namesake: Reverend John Davenport, founder of New Haven

Mascot: The gnome, a three-foot-tall wooden, um, gnome, that a student brought back from the California redwood forest in 1998. (Stealing, painting, and otherwise defacing the gnome is a popular pastime for non–D-porters.)

Pros: Waterford crystal chandelier in the dining hall! How chic!

Cons: The architecture. Gothic on the outside, colonial on the inside. How gauche!

Notable Architecture and Features

The Cottage: A separate little brick house in one corner of the courtyard. Groups of six seniors actually campaign to live here and are voted on by their class.

Thanks to recent renovations, D-port shares a basement recreation complex with Pierson, which, unfortunately, is its hated archrival.

Events and Customs

Diveball: A game played on the pool table down in the Buttery (known as the "Dive"). Accounts of the rules vary—you'll have to go down and check it out for yourself.

The Porn Party: A pornography-themed party at the cottage. Known for the . . . interesting wallpaper. Dress as your favorite porn character for a discount.

Ezra Stiles

Namesake: The Reverend Ezra Stiles (1727–1795), an early president of Yale and dedicated supporter of the Revolution. He is remembered for requiring all Yale students to learn Hebrew because of a dream he had in which he was denied access to heaven for not speaking the language.

Mascot: The A. Bartlett Giamatti Memorial Moose, the stuffed head of which gazes mournfully out over the dining hall.

Pros: Stiles has dominated the Tyng Cup race more often than not recently.

Cons: You can't live in a suite, which means no common rooms.

Notable Architecture and Features

Stiles (and Morse), which were designed in the sixties by famed Finnish architect Ero Saarinen, have no horizontal right angles anywhere in the building. You'll learn this when you try putting your bed against the wall.

In the basement, you'll find the Stiles Little Theater, much beloved of improv groups. Stiles doesn't have suites, so the Stilesians throw their parties in the little theater instead.

Events and Customs

Arts Festival: The dining hall, the master's house, and even the courtyard are turned into galleries for gifted Stilesians.

Jonathan Edwards

Namesake: Jonathan Edwards (1703–1758), terrifying fundamentalist minister

Mascot: The spider. Jonathan Edwards wrote a treatise on spiders at the tender age of twelve.

Pros: JE has more money than any other college, the result of a large endowment donated right before Yale outlawed donations to a specific college.

Cons: The rooms are notoriously tiny, especially the group known as the "sophomore slums."

Notable Architecture and Features
JE is rich, but kind of ugly.

Events and Customs
Spider Ball: A formal dance open only to JE students and their dates. Rumor has it that the alcohol budget alone is more than some colleges have for all their social events combined.

Culture Draw: Thanks to JE's overstuffed coffers, frequent drawings are held for all-expense-paid trips to plays, operas, and swanky restaurants in New York.

Tulip Day: A fall event in which students plant tulips for the coming spring, carve pumpkins, and drink cider.

Wet Monday: The Monday after Easter, the freshman attack their elders in JE with squirt guns in a massive all-day water war. (Used to be the other way around, until one year they caused thousands of dollars in water damage to Farnam.)

Morse

Namesake: Samuel Morse (1791–1872), inventor of the telegraph

Mascot: The axe. Or occasionally the walrus. (The current master thinks that the axe is too violent, and "Morse" is French for *walrus*.)

Pros: If you win the room draw, you can live in the penthouse double: a two-story room on the top of the Morse tower with a private bathroom (with tub) and access to a rooftop terrace.

Cons: Morse's notoriously stupid housing draw is too complex to describe here.

Notable Architecture and Features
Each student in Morse (and Stiles) gets one college-issued chair in their dorm room. The interesting part is that the windows were designed to be just slightly narrower than the college-issued chair, so that in case of riot the students would not be able to throw the chairs out the windows. Morse and Stiles were built in 1961, at which time this sort of thing was a serious concern.

Party suite: The Sexplex. Not really a suite, to be sure, but six people who live on a hall.

Events and Customs
Casino Night: A giant formal party that Morse and Stiles throw for the whole campus, with gaming tables, a live band, and even pretty ladies walking around selling cigars. You will hear many times that *Rolling Stone* once selected this as one of the top college parties in the country . . . although no one remembers when.

Pierson

Namesake: Abraham Pierson Jr. (1641–1707), Yale's first rector

Mascot: None. Presumably, Pierson is above this sort of thing.

Pros: Two Piersonites organized a legendary prank at the 2005 Harvard-Yale game. (They convinced the entire Harvard side to hold up placards with giant letters that spelled out "We Suck.")

Cons: The dining hall is self-serve. This can be nice for a change, and I suppose it's all very democratic, but still. It's not like Piersonites are paying less for their room and board.

Notable Architecture and Features

Pierson technically has a gate on York Street, despite being tucked away behind the Drama school. A long, long walkway stretches down the flank of Davenport into the Pierson courtyard. But since you have to swipe past the gate to enter the walkway, it counts as part of the Pierson courtyard. Also, Pierson has a clock tower modeled after Independence Hall. Pretty weird, huh?

In the basement of Pierson, you can find Niko's, a music café. Several colleges have theatre spaces, so it's nice to see a specifically musical venue.

There's a modernist sculpture in the courtyard that you can reach up and spin around as you walk past.

Events and Customs

Pierson Day: If you don't want to get thrown into a pit of Pierson-yellow jello, you'd better be elsewhere. The master and dean often show up and take all comers.

The Tuesday Night Club: A regular party every Tuesday night in the lower courtyard.

Saybrook

Namesake: Old Saybrook, Connecticut, where Yale was founded

Mascot: the seal

Pros: It's the largest college (by population).

Cons: No one *really* gets naked during the Saybrook Strip (see below). What kind of tradition is that?

Notable Architecture and Features

In the common room, there's a scale model of the whole college. Sadly, the windows are painted over, so you can't see if it contains a miniature model of the model.

The Saybrook party suite is called the twelve-pack, a mammoth complex for twelve sophomores in Wrexham Tower.

The Saybrook basement contains a *massive hoard of silver bullion*. It's been a tradition since the founding of the college for Saybrook alums to make gifts of silver (candlesticks, etc.) to the college. Some of this is displayed in the master's house, some of it . . . well, it would be irresponsible to start an unfounded rumor that it's hidden behind a false wall near the Saybrook darkroom. So we won't.

Events and Customs

Saybrook Strip: The traditional third-quarter disrobing at Yale football games. The Yale band used to play "The Stripper" while this was going on, but eventually the powers that be forced them to stop. The Saybrugians go ahead and (don't) strip anyway.

Saye and Sele Day: End of the school year outdoor BBQ bash.

The Saybrook seal (not the animal, the sigil) is engraved on a stone circle near one of the gates. Supposedly if you step on it, you'll never graduate. This tradition is similar to, but not as famous as, the Branford Gate. In some ways it's better, in that you can actually *do* it without cutting an inch-thick bolt.

Silliman

Namesake: Benjamin Silliman (1779–1864), Yale's first professor of chemistry and natural history (one of the first in the country)

Mascot: the salamander

Pros: It's the biggest college (in terms of real estate, at least). Size does matter. It's so big that occasionally people wind up living two people to a three-person suite.

Cons: Freshmen Sillimanders also live in Silliman. To upperclassmen, this is a point of pride, but most of the Silliman frosh will tell you that they feel just a little bit screwed.

Notable Architecture and Features

The Beach Club, which has a weekly "Tequila Monday."

There is a climbing wall in the Silliman basement for all the little Sillimanders to hone their skills.

Events and Customs

Safety Dance: The annual eighties boogaloo, a campuswide attraction.

Frosh Olympics: The frosh entryways compete against each other in things like musical chairs, shoving marshmallows into their mouths, and, of course, slurping up condiments and spitting them into a cup.

Richfest: A year-end party somehow inspired by Rich Marshall, class of '96. We have no idea who he is, but he must have been a hell of a guy.

Timothy Dwight

Namesake: Timothy Dwight IV (1752–1817), and/or Timothy Dwight V (1828–1916), both presidents of the university during their time

Mascot: *Technically* the lion; *actually* the bell (see below for more about the bell)

Pros: The TD master, Robert Farris Thompson, is a living legend—even students from other residential colleges address him as "Master T." An expert on Afro-Caribbean culture, he routinely flies in exotic dancers from all over the world to perform at parties.

Cons: It's far from everything. Said one TD student: "I think it's technically in a different city. Get a bike."

Notable Architecture and Features

The fourth-floor suites in entryways F, G, and H are connected by a balcony, so seniors can visit each other sans stairs.

Party suite: the sextet in Rosenfeld Hall (TD's annex space above the language lab). Recently dubbed BaRH (say it "Bar H").

Events and Customs

Near-worship of the bell: Timothy Dwight has a bell. It's just what you'd think: a big ol' bell they take around and ring at sporting events, intramurals, traffic jams . . . To say that TD students are attached to it would be an understatement.

The Chubb Fellowships: Big shots from all walks of life spend the day hanging out with lucky TD students. More importantly, they do it at New Haven's nicest restaurants.

TDDDTD Day: TD Drunk During the Day Day, which is held on the last day of classes spring semester. Speaks for itself.

Llamaland: One of the TD fellows owns one of the old Rockefeller estates in upstate New York, and in September all the freshman go up there for a day of bucolic, llama-filled splendor.

Trumbull

Namesake: John Trumbull (1756–1843), governor of Connecticut during the Revolutionary War

Mascot: the bull

Pros: James Gamble Rogers, who designed nine of the residential colleges, considered Trumbull to be his masterpiece. And newly renovated for 2006, it now features three-pronged outlets. Ooooh.

Cons: Trumbull is the poorest college. It can't even afford a fourth wall, instead sharing one with Sterling.

Notable Architecture and Features

The potty court gargoyle, perched on what is unmistakably a wee stone toilet, is repainted every year by the senior class.

In the basement, you'll find both the Nick Chapel (one of the most sought-after theater spaces on campus) and the Trumbull Art Space.

Events and Customs

Pamplona: Competitions, free T-shirts, and the roasting of an entire pig. Ole!

The Rumble in Trumbull: Settle your grudges in the ring (with pillows, sumo suits, or giant boxing gloves).

Trum' Crier: A horned figure who appears in the dining hall to make announcements or at least to report that "It's six o'clock, and all is well!"

Poker games go on all over campus, but the one in Trumbull has a buy-in of hundreds of dollars, and has even been mentioned in *Sports Illustrated*.

CHAPTER
Ten

Around noon, Nina and I met up at the gym. The Kiphuth Trophy Room was larger than I'd expected—perhaps not surprising given that some of its contents dated from the 1840s. Inside the hard-carved oak cases were not only trophies commemorating Yale's glorious **football history** but also baseballs, pieces of boats, uniforms, and, of course, Handsome Dan I.

Luckily for us, not too many people bother to visit; everyone's too busy taking classes in Tango or **Swedish massage**. The place was empty. I stood lookout while Nina jimmied the glass case open.

"Your turn," she whispered, taking my place at the door.

Gingerly, I lifted Dan and crawled underneath the conference table with him. He stared back at me with a bull-doggy grin that said, "Yes, I'm dead. What of it?"

football history: Football was pretty much invented at Yale by Walter Camp, class of 1880. For many decades, Yale was a football powerhouse; legendary Notre Dame coach Knute Rockne once bragged that he got all of his plays from us. But when the Ivy League agreed not to give athletic scholarships, Yale football fumbled its way into irrelevance.

Swedish massage: The gym offers a wide variety of courses, for a small fee. You don't get any credit, but you can learn to scuba dive, kickbox, or tie flies (for fishin'). Beware of signing up for any ballroom dance class with a significant other, unless you're sure you'll still be dating in eight weeks.

> **Art and Architecture building:** A shining example of "Brutalist" architecture, the façade of the A&A building looks like corrugated cardboard. It seems designed for the sole purpose of inspiring the students to create something—anything!—better.

*Why can't a clue be somewhere romantic, I thought, like the roof of the **Art and Architecture building**?*

I reached into my backpack and pulled out the scalpel Nina had liberated from her bio lab. Running my free hand over Dan's flanks, I wondered how I could get in there with a minimal amount of mess. I flipped him onto his side and inspected his, um, haunches. There was a four-inch incision sewn up with large black stitches.

My mom always wanted me to be a doctor. But somehow I don't think "Miles Bowman, Veterinarian Proctologist" is what she had in mind.

"Are you sure you don't want to do the honors?" I yelled out to Nina.

"Positive," she said from the door. I could see her feet shuffling.

"Maybe we can get your boyfriend to do it," I teased her.

She laughed. "Somehow I don't think this is up Perfect Paul's alley."

I gasped. "You call him that too?"

"*You* call him that too?" she said in astonishment, ducking down to look at me.

"Yeah, it's my secret nickname for him," I admitted, a little embarrassed. "Well, me and pretty much everyone in our freshman entryway. I'm a little surprised that *you* would use it, though."

She looked embarrassed too. "I like him and all, but sometimes . . . sometimes I catch myself staring at him, just waiting for him to make a mistake."

CHAPTER TEN

"Don't hold your breath" I grinned at her.

"Honestly," she laughed, standing back up. "He's like a Stepford Boyfriend."

Feeling better, I began to cut.

Thankfully, whatever twisted fiend had hidden the clue inside the dead bulldog hadn't put it very far inside—I only had to poke an inch into the sawdust before a rolled slip of parchment fell out onto the carpet.

"Nina! I got it!"

She crawled under the table and scooted next to me as I opened it:

This even-handed justice
Commends th' ingredience of our poison'd chalice
To our own lips.

Macbeth
Act II, scene iii, line 20

"Huh," I frowned. "The Scottish play."

"Oh, you're an actor?"

"Well, I dabble," I said modestly. "Deep down, I think I've always wanted to be a playwright, ever since my high school drama teacher—"

"So what does this mean?" she asked.

"Well," I said, in my making-a-smart-comment-in-section voice, "Macbeth is clearly wrestling with the twin demons of ambition and—"

"No," she said patiently. "What does the *clue* mean?"

"Oh," I said. "Nope. No idea. You?"

She shrugged. "I was always in the band in high school."

We stared at it. "Did I mention that Macbeth is wrestling with the twin demons of—"

"Hello?" said someone by the door. "Is anyone in here?"

I looked down the length of the conference table to see shiny leather shoes that could only be security guard issue. I froze. Any second he was going to see the open case and the missing bulldog. Dean Sheely would be the least of my problems once generations of die-hard alumni heard about this.

Suddenly, Nina moaned, loudly. It wasn't the kind of moan you make out of despair. I looked at her in surprise just as she threw her arms around my neck and crushed her lips to mine. A part of me continued to panic, but most of me forgot about the security guard and the mutilated bulldog behind me and just concentrated on how her kiss was precisely like I'd imagined it.

"Hey!" said the security guard. Nina recoiled in embarrassment as he scowled at us, kneeling at the head of the table. "What are you two kids doing down there?"

"I'm sorry," she stuttered. "My boyfriend's in town but my roommate won't let us have the room. Can we just have five minutes?"

The security guard's scowl and Nina's trembly pout battled for a moment, but Nina's pout was an undefeated world champion. The guard smiled. "Five minutes," he said, and he walked out and closed the door.

I squeezed Nina's hand gratefully. She smiled back at me.

"That was a close call," I said. "I owe you one."

"Think nothing of it. So?"

"So what?"

"Aren't you going to finish what you started?"

CHAPTER TEN

"You kissed ME!" is what I almost said. But then I realized she was talking about the bulldog. Gritting my teeth, I fished into my backpack for the needle and thread I'd picked up at the bookstore.

Nina was copying the clue into a notepad. "You want your own copy?" she asked me.

"Act two, scene three, line twenty," I told her. "I have a good memory. My drama teacher once said—"

"Good. So we can put the clue back in the bulldog."

I looked at her incredulously. "You're kidding, right? What would be the point of that?"

"It just feels wrong to take it. This clue's been hidden here for decades. To just destroy all that work . . ."

I handed her the needle. "Tell you what: *you* sew it in there; *I'll* stand guard."

She looked at it miserably. "Do I have to?"

"I thought you were premed!"

"Not anymore!"

A little later we headed down **Jock Walk** together. The adrenaline rush from our close call with the guard had warn off, and the furtive kiss we'd shared was weighing heavily on both of our minds. Well. *My* mind anyway. But Nina sure seemed pensive about something.

"Listen, Miles," she said, "that kiss—"

Jock Walk: The crooked pathway between Morse and Stiles, so called because it leads to the gym.

"That was quick thinking!" I blurted out. "I can't believe the guard fell for it though—he needs to watch more movies."

Something like relief washed over Nina's face. "It was all I could think of on short notice." Then she frowned, as if she didn't like the way that sounded. "I mean, it's not like I *wanted* to do that."

"No no," I said reassuringly. "Why would you? I mean, you have a boyfriend."

"That's what I meant," she said. "Well, I'm glad it's not going to make things weird."

"Weird? Nah, I've already forgotten it."

We walked the rest of the way back to Stiles in silence. At the gate to the college, she paused while I fished out my **ID card**.

I took a breath. "So hey, it's Friday."

"Yeah? So?"

"Well, the ***Herald***t out. If you're not busy, I was thinking we could grab dinner and check out the **comic strips**. An awesome mystery-solving team like us, maybe we can figure out what one of them means."

"Right, because we were so successful at figuring out what that Shakespeare quote means," she said sourly.

"Hey, cheer up. I bet you this is a good thing—the clues are getting trickier because we're closer to the end. We'll figure it out eventually, just give it time."

ID card: A Yale student ID card will be your lifeline: it serves as house key, library card, and meal ticket. The one thing it's not good for is identification: try using this at a bar and the bouncer will laugh in your face.

***Herald*:** The *Herald* is a mixed bag. Its news section tends to go in depth about things its readers couldn't care less about, like what the Yale Corporation does. On the other hand, the sidebars and columns usually make for good light reading, and the arts and entertainment section has solid reviews of everything from student plays to Hollywood movies.

comic strips: The *Herald* has a long tradition of surrealistic, incomprehensible, and occasionally disturbing comics. Every now and then they'll get a funny one too, but that's clearly not their goal.

"You're probably right . . ." she trailed off. "I should really go and pack now."

But she didn't move. She parted her lips slightly. I could still taste the cherry-flavored gloss she was wearing. My breath caught in my throat. Too tired for self-control, I leaned in to gently brush my lips against hers.

"What are you doing?" she said, pulling away.

"Nothing," I mumbled pointlessly, since it was an obvious lie.

"Why did you . . . I told you it was only a distraction!" Her shock and anger were unbearable.

"I just thought, you know," I said lamely, wanting to sink into the flagstones. "Never mind, I just read your signals wrong . . ."

"I wasn't sending any signals!" she snapped.

"I know that! Now."

A guy with a lacrosse stick walked through the gate, looking at us curiously.

Nina took a deep breath. "Miles, if you've been following me around because you thought we might become some kind of an item—"

It was my turn to be indignant. "Following you around? Hey, who got us up to the top of Sterling?"

"Gary."

"Who happens to be *my* friend!"

"Listen, you said you were against this from the very beginning," she snapped. "So why don't you just stop?" She turned and hurried toward Broadway.

"At first!" I said, hurrying after her. "I didn't want to do this at first. But now I'm in too deep. Somewhere out there is a fabulous treasure and a murderer, and I'm not going to be satisfied until I find both."

She stopped outside the bookstore and shook her head sadly. "I never meant to lead you on, Miles. I'm sorry." She walked away again, and this time I didn't follow.

"I'll call you when we get back from break?" I said. "To talk about the clue?"

"Don't bother, Miles," she said over her shoulder. "You don't have to put up with my escapades anymore." And she rounded the corner taking the clue with her.

Know Your Dans

Handsome Dan, the Yale Bulldog, was the first mascot of any University in America. And they just keep on getting handsomer . . .

Handsome Dan I: Served 1889–1898. "In personal appearance, he seemed like a cross between an alligator and a horned frog," wrote the *Hartford Courant* in his eulogy. "He was always taken to games on a leash, and the Harvard football team for years owed its continued existence to the fact that the rope held."

Handsome Dan II: Served 1933–1937. In a heart-warming Depression era tale, this Dan was bought with pennies donated by the freshman class. Awww. He was kidnapped by Harvard in 1934, on the eve of The Game. Gasp! Yale still won, 14-0, and the dog was returned. Huzzah!

Handsome Dan III: Served 1937–1938. Probably the worst Handsome Dan ever, this dog turned out to be afraid of crowds and was retired without having mascotted a single game. C'mon, selection committee, do your homework.

Handsome Dan IX: Served 1953–1959. This Dan graced the cover of *Sports Illustrated* in November, 1956, something we can be reasonably sure will never happen again. In 1954 he fell off the dock at the Yale Boathouse and nearly drowned. He actually had to be resuscitated. Mouth to mouth with a bulldog: that's school spirit.

Handsome Dan X: Served 1959–1969. A real winner, he not only presided over the football team's undefeated season of 1960, he once won "Best Bulldog" at the Cape Cod Kennel Club Dog Show and placed in the Non-Sporting Group Competition.

Handsome Dan XII: Served 1975–1984. This Dan was a Danielle, a female bulldog in honor of Yale's finally letting women in. She was described by her owner as "pugnacious and stubborn, but lovable." To what degree this description can be applied to Yale women in general, it's probably best not to ask.

Handsome Dan XIII: Served 1984–1996. Perhaps the greatest Dan since Dans began, he could sing along with the fight song (sort of), play dead when asked if he'd rather die or join Harvard, and viciously attack any other mascot, even chasing a few Princeton cheerleaders into the stands. He was once ejected from the Yale-Harvard Game for mistakenly attacking a mounted policeman.

Handsome Dan XV: Served 1996–2005. With a white "Y" naturally appearing in his fur, he seemed chosen by fate. He appeared on *Animal Planet*, graced the cover of *Dog Owner* magazine, and was once a clue on *Jeopardy*. Extremely docile, he was mobbed by children everywhere he went, like a valuable Pokemon.

Handsome Dan XVI: Chosen April 2005 during Spring Fling, "Mugsy" beat out nine other dogs to be crowned the new Handsome Dan. The deciding factor was the way he mauled a Crimson flag that was presented to him (never mind that dogs are colorblind).

CHAPTER
Eleven

The night before **the Game** is the biggest party night of the year. Your fellow Elis are all officially on Thanksgiving break, your alumni friends are back in town, and you might even have a few **Cantabs** you're glad to see. I'd been planning to meet some friends for pizza before heading over to the big Yale–Harvard dance party at **Toad's**, but after what had happened with Nina, I didn't feel like celebrating, or even talking to anyone. And because I knew that if I ate at the Stiles dining hall a dozen friends would come up and ask me what was wrong, I went to Calhoun to eat alone. I had a big bowl of pudding and read the ***Record*** in the hopes it would raise my spirits. It didn't.

But when I went back to my room after dinner, there was someone there waiting for me, reading my email. The first

The Game: The annual season-ending football matchup between Harvard and Yale. Outsiders refer to it as the Yale–Harvard Game—to students of either school, it's just "The Game."

Cantabs: Short for "Cantabrigians" (Harvard is in Cambridge, MA, and "Cantabrigian" is an old timey way of saying "dude from Cambridge."). Harvard doesn't have an official mascot, so they're referred to as the "Crimson" or the "Cantabs." Or just the "Losers."

Toad's: This nationally famous rock club is located in the center of the Yale campus. It's hard to think of an act that hasn't played Toad's at some point, from the Wu-Tang Clan, to George Clinton, and even the Rolling Stones (don't hold your breath—it was just once, and unannounced).

Record: The *Yale Record*, the nation's oldest and at one time most respected humor magazine, suffered a sad decline in the 1970s, somehow allowing the *Harvard Lampoon* to steal its reputation as top dog. But in recent years, the *Record* has come roaring back, producing six issues a year, which are actually pretty funny.

CHAPTER ELEVEN | 100

thing I noticed was a black fedora, the same one I'd seen on the birdwatcher from Sterling. The figure slowly turned toward me.

"You!" I exclaimed.

"Hey Miles," said Jessica Shechner. "Nice place. Very cozy."

I stood rooted in the doorframe.

"You've been following me! Why? What do you want?"

She calmly reached into a coat pocket and pulled out a handgun. She didn't bother pointing it at me, but she didn't really have to. "I want you to come with me," she said. "Some of my friends are waiting to meet you."

I had a brief vision of my body being buried beneath **Beinecke Plaza**. "Okay," I said. Numbly, I stepped back into the hall.

"Actually . . ." said Shechner, "you're going to need to dress up first."

* * * * *

I'd never seen **Mory's** full before, but it was the night before the Game, and generations of Yalies had converged to celebrate in style. There were grizzled old men who could have been classmates with Monty Burns, professors drinking alongside their students, and even the **Whiffenpoofs** singing "**Boola Boola**." Although the dress code no longer requires jackets and ties, most of the patrons were traditionalists,

---

Bienecke Plaza: The granite-paved area bordered by the Bienecke Rare Book Library, Commons, Woolsey, and Wall Street.

Mory's: Mory's is a private club, but since it will admit pretty much anyone with a Yale connection, it's got over 18,000 members. Various extracurricular groups still make traditional weekly outings.

Whiffenpoofs: The Whiffenpoofs are the nation's oldest collegiate a cappella group, and still one of the best. Rising male seniors from the other a cappella groups try out for the Whiffs, and the best.

Boola Boola: One of Yale's fight songs. It's unclear what "Boola" is supposed to mean, but one theory is that it's the sound produced when a drunk Yalie tries to sing "Bulldog," another of Yale's fight songs.

so even though I'd been marched there at gunpoint I was glad I'd managed to find my blazer. The smell of **rarebit** hung in the air, ancient framed photos hung on the walls, and signed oars hung from the ceiling.

Jessica followed me up the creaky stairs. The second floor was for private parties, and waiters went back and forth between the rooms bringing fresh **toasting** cups and removing the empties.

As we approached, I began to hear the sound of drunken singing: "Halleluuuu-JAH, sing Halleluuu-JAH, put a nickel on the drum, save another **drunken bum**!" Jessica gave the old "shave and a haircut" knock. After a moment, she realized there was no chance anyone had heard her and went ahead and opened the door herself.

Ten people were singing and pounding on the wooden table, while one was rubbing the giant toasting cup upside down on his head to clean off the rim. The guy sitting next to him unfolded a white paper napkin and laid it down in front of him. Everyone slowed down for the big finish (except for two people busy drinking other cups). "Put a nickel on the druuum . . . " The man with the cup

rarebit: Mory's still offers the four items that were on its menu when it opened in 1861: sardines, eggs on toast, Welsh rarebit (a thick slab of bread submerged in a cheese and beer sauce), and golden buck (the former, with a poached egg).

toasting: Toasting sessions are the reason most people go to Mory's. You and your chums reserve a private room and spend the evening passing around "cups," making elaborate toasts and singing songs. The Mory's cups are no ordinary cups. They are the Humvees of drinking vessels: impressive, expensive, and bigger than anyone really needs. They look like tremendous silver trophies and hold easily two pitchers of liquid. To finish one, you'll need about five friends.

drunken bum: The traditional Mory's drinking song, actually an old Salvation Army song, a fact that few Yalies are aware of, even though many shop at the Salvation Army (see page 109).

Assassins: Every college has its own version of this game. You have to hunt down a series of randomly assigned players and "kill" them with a squirt or dart gun, while keeping an eye out for your own would-be killer.

Pundits: A sort of mock secret society dedicated to the performing of pranks. Recently, they recorded the audio from a porn movie and played it through the speakers of a lecture hall during a class, and they famously almost got onto the *Today* show while impersonating the Whiffenpoofs.

candy-throwing people: Each semester, the night before finals begin, the Pundits toss aside all semblance of secrecy (and all articles of clothing), and march through the library, bagpipes blaring, handing out candy to wearily cramming students.

placed it upside down on the napkin and put a hand on top. Everyone leaned in to place their hands over his. "Annnd . . . yooou'll . . . beee . . . saaaaaved!" As they finished, the cup was lifted. A cheer erupted as someone waved the spotless napkin aloft.

As everyone sat down, they finally seemed to notice me. A large bearded man at the head of the table laughed. "I don't believe he fell for it!"

"Fell for what?" I frowned, turning to Jessica. She smiled and pulled the gun out of her coat. I desperately threw myself under the table as she pulled the trigger—sending a stream of water into my terrified face. The crowd guffawed.

"Ezra Stiles **Assassins** champion, three years running!" she smirked. "Bang. You're dead."

"To Jessica!" said the student holding the toasting cup, just before he drank.

"To Jessica!" they all repeated boisterously.

"Sit down," said the bearded man, as I resentfully got to my feet.

"I'd rather stand," I said.

The big man considered this for a minute. "Why?" he finally asked.

"It's meant to be a gesture of mistrust."

"Ah. Well, we're all very humbled. I'm Josh McNeil, Lord High Executioner of the **Pundits**."

"The Pundits!" I exclaimed. "You pull all this cloak-and-dagger nonsense to get me here, and it turns out you're the **candy-throwing people**?"

CHAPTER ELEVEN

"So you know our work?" said McNeil with a grin. There was a pause as a waiter brought in a **red cup**.

"What have you heard," said McNeil, once the waiter was out of earshot, "about the Eli Opal?"

I decided to sit down after all and put my cards on the table. "I know what Professor Quinlan published about it. Benjamin Silliman had it in Philadelphia, but it never made it back to campus. Maybe you could tell me how a clue to its whereabouts wound up in the binding of a two-hundred-year-old jokebook?"

McNeil cleared his throat. "You're familiar with James Fenimore Cooper, the novelist?"

"Sure. How does he relate to this?"

"We consider him the first Pundit."

The girl currently holding the cup exclaimed, "To James Fenimore Cooper!"

"J! F! C!" yelled the rest of the Pundits. "Finger lickin' good!" She drank as they pounded on the table in approval.

I ignored this. "I didn't know he was a Yale graduate."

"He wasn't," said Shechner. "He was expelled."

"For what?"

"The official explanation? Pranks," said McNeil. "He once taught a donkey to sit in a **professor's chair**."

"I'm guessing there's an unofficial explanation . . ."

> **red cup:** You order cups by color (the ingredients are a closely kept secret). Unfortunately (or fortunately, if you're reading this out loud to your parents), if your group has a substantial number of students under twenty-one, they'll insist that you get a bunch of nonalcoholic "Imperial" cups, which are basically filled with very expensive Hawaiian Punch.

> **professor's chair:** This is actually true, believe it or not. But the rest of this bit is lies.

"When Silliman was making his triumphant return to Connecticut with his wagon of gems, Cooper, then a sophomore, went to meet him in Manhattan. They opened up a tab at a tavern. When Silliman awoke the next afternoon with a splitting headache, Cooper was long gone."

"And so was the Opal?" I guessed.

"Correct. Cooper denied knowing anything about it, but they expelled him anyway."

"Wrongfully accused, eh?"

"Are you kidding? He *totally* stole it," laughed Shechner. "Kept it his whole life as a memento. And before he died, he gave it to a group of students for safekeeping."

"The first Pundits," said McNeil.

"To us!" shouted a tall blonde whom I recognized from a **Fifth Humour** show. She tilted the cup back until the purple liquid dripped down her chin.

"Cooper said that as long as the gem was on Yale's campus," said McNeil solemnly, "the true spirit of the university would survive."

This seemed a little too saccharine for this bunch. "Really?" I asked.

"Also, as long as the gem remains hidden, the Pundits receive one-tenth of the royalties from The Last of the Mohicans."

"To Daniel Day Lewis!" said the guy with the cup. Everyone cheered.

"And the clues?" I asked.

Fifth Humour: Want to do comedy, but too slow for improv? The Fifth Humour performs scripted skits—like *Saturday Night Live*, except funny, and with cursing.

"That was Cooper's idea too. He donated his copy of The *Philogelos* to the Yale Library, with the first clue glued inside the front cover. He left instructions that every ten years or so, a Pundit has to get the book, rip the cover open, and create a new set of clues in new locations."

"But *why*? What's the point?"

McNeil shrugged. "It's what Cooper told us to do. We *are* a secret society. Blind adherence to tradition comes with the territory."

I shook my head. "So you mean all those clues I've been running around after are only ten years old?"

"Well, more like thirty," said McNeil. "In the mid-seventies, the Pundits chose a Berkeley senior to set up the new hunt. To his horror, he discovered that Cooper's book was missing. He tried to contact the last person who replaced the clues, only to find out that he had died of liver failure." He took the toasting cup and stood up to make a toast. "And the Pundit who discovered that the book was missing was Jeremiah Quinlan."

"To Professor Quinlan!" exclaimed several Pundits, but there were scattered mutters of discontent. I looked at Jessica.

"Quinlan isn't . . . well, wasn't . . . exactly popular with other Pundits," she explained. "Years after he graduated, he began to think the Opal never should have been hidden in the first place. Even though he left us out of that article, he wasn't exactly discrete. When you told me you were going to see him about a jokebook, I almost tackled you. I was sure he'd bring the gem right to the Peabody. Not that I wanted him to fall off Harkness, or anything," she added quickly.

Which brought us to the big question: "So why are you telling me this?" I asked.

"That gem wasn't meant to be found," said McNeil. "It's supposed to stay hidden."

"I followed you for three days, hoping you'd get stuck somewhere and give up," said Shechner, "but it looks like you actually might succeed."

"And so you decided to threaten Nina and steal my library books?" I asked, annoyed.

She looked shocked. "Somebody stole your library books? That's not a prank. That's just mean. And who's Nina?"

Her reaction gave me pause. I couldn't see what she'd have to gain by lying. But if the Pundits hadn't taken the books, who had? "I may have left them at Starbucks," I said cautiously. "Nina is . . . a barista there."

McNeil cleared his throat. "Let's cut the crap," he said. "We want you to give the book back to us and promise that you'll stop looking for the gem."

I took a moment to stare at the decades-old initials carved into the wooden table. I believed their story, as far as it went, but I wasn't about to sell Nina out like that.

"And what if I refuse?" I asked.

"Then we call upon you the Great Prank," said McNeil ominously.

"The what?"

"There are hundreds of Pundits all over the world. We will tell each and every one of them to prank you back to the Stone Age."

"Dozens of unordered pizzas arriving at your house. Your underwear scattered to the four winds," said Jessica.

CHAPTER ELEVEN

"Your toilet seats forever covered with Vaseline. The hoods of your automobiles forever festooned with bologna," added the blonde.

"And wherever you go," said McNeil, "you and your descendents will be forever plagued by laughing voices asking if your refrigerator is running."

I stared at them. "Have you ever actually done this before?"

"Nope," admitted McNeil. "We'd kind of like to try it, actually."

"Okay," I said. "You win. I'll give you the clue. I just need to go back to my room and get it."

"Tomomi, go with him," said McNeil. A petite Asian girl stood up and smoothed down her dress. "Ah, but where are my manners?" McNeil continued. "One for the road?" He handed me the cup.

Everyone looked at me, waiting for a toast. The first thing that came into my head was, "You are all idiots." I went with the second thing that came into my head, which seemed appropriate: "This even-handed justice commends the ingredients of our poisoned chalice to our own lips."

"*Macbeth*," nodded McNeil as I raised the cup. "Act one, scene seven."

I stopped on the verge of drinking. "Are you sure it's not act two?"

"Positive," he said. "I took two semesters of **Bloom**."

"Drink!" screamed an impatient guy to my right, so I did.

Bloom: Harold Bloom, the world's foremost Shakespeare scholar. He publishes a book every four months and never stops rubbing his shoulder. Go ahead and ask him about the Leonardo DiCaprio *Romeo and Juliet* and see what happens to you.

Really Off-Campus

Sketchy New Haven Places to Go

Mory's is one of New Haven's more illustrious nightspots. But maybe illustrious isn't what you're looking for. If that's the case, consider the following destinations.

Sports Haven

New Haven's premiere off-track betting facility, Sports Haven features many grizzled old men with mustaches and cigarettes. You'll go with your friends and spend twenty minutes failing to figure out how to read a racing form before betting the two-dollar minimum on the horse with the silliest name.

Salvation Army

Here, hipsters from Greenwich obliviously shop for irony next to welfare moms. Perhaps a charitable organization can't really be "sketchy," but there's definitely something disturbing about a display window that juxtaposes Barbie dolls with no legs, Amiga computers, and a solitary sequined cowboy boot.

Catwalk

New Haven's premier fully nude, no-contact adult go-go dancing establishment. No liquor is served; you have to get hammered at the bar next door. And trust us, you will need to get hammered first. Ask for "Ice," and offer her a matchbook. We dare you.

The Owl Shop

A real straight-up old-timey smoke shoppe. Fred, one of the world's top pipe repairmen, has been working there almost fifty years. Joe, who creates custom tobacco blends for the connoisseurs, is a rookie, with only forty years.

Alternate Universe

Best . . . comic book store . . . ever! You thought you were embarrassed when you met your TA in the Catwalk? Wait until he catches you picking up your back issues of *Namor the Sub-Mariner*. Try passing *that* off as research.

The Edge Tattoo Parlor

Yale's tattoo and body piercing mecca. For some reason, it has the Mortal Kombat logo in the window.

CHAPTER
Twelve

I had no intention of letting the Pundits have the clue. First of all, I didn't physically have it (I had it memorized, but they didn't need to know that). Secondly, even though Nina had told me she didn't want me involved, I wasn't ready to give up. Besides, these guys didn't scare me. I was pretty sure the minds behind the Great Prank hadn't murdered anyone. That meant there was someone else out there who had. I felt a lot less expendable knowing that Nina and I were the only ones who knew the next clue.

I eyed my escort warily. She smiled reassuringly. At least she wasn't too upset to have been pulled away from her toasting session.

"Tomomi," I said. "What is that, a Korean name?"

"Japanese."

"And, uh, you're supposed to stop me if I run?"

"That's the idea." I looked at her again. Even in her platform heels, she only came up to my shoulder.

"So, you know karate, or something?" I asked.

She stopped in her tracks. "What, just because I'm from Japan I'm supposed to know martial arts? No, my parents are paranoid, so they bought me a Taser."

"I'm sorry, I just—"

"Just shut up and lead me to your room. And you'd better not live -in TD, or I'll Tase you."

She didn't know what college I was in. That made things easier. "Oh no," I said. "It's not far at all . . ."

Well, I certainly wasn't going to take her to where I *actually* lived. We were going to D-Port.

On any given Friday night, the **Davenport Cottage** is a pretty tremendous place to lose somebody, but the Friday before the Game it was Mardi Gras. Most of the crowd was outside by necessity, and even the courtyard barely seemed big enough. There was a band set up on the patio, and the Cottage's residents made the rounds with trays of shrimp. Once I'd forced my way inside, with Tomomi right behind me, I pushed through the crowd surrounding the kegs.

"It's in here," I told her, pointing to a random bedroom. "I'll just be a minute. Play some **Beer Pong** while you're waiting." I went in and slammed the door. There was a couple making out on top of a giant mound of coats, but they didn't look up. I opened a window and climbed onto the roof of the porch. A hundred people stared up at me from the courtyard.

Davenport Cottage: Many colleges have party suites, but the Davenport Cottage is a campus-wide destination. It's a separate brick building in a corner of the courtyard with a built-in bar. Groups of six (guys or girls) actually have to campaign for the suite, and the entire class of rising Davenport seniors votes on who they want to bear the awesome responsibility of rocking their worlds.

Beer Pong: Drinking games are a ubiquitous part of college life. Beirut, Flipcup, Quarters . . . there are hundreds of them, but they all seem to involve manipulation of the (equally ubiquitous) big red plastic cups used at parties.

"Go Yale!" I screamed. They all cheered.

I lowered myself down to the ground and headed for the gate. Over my shoulder, I saw Tomomi looking out one of the Cottage's windows in dismay. I hoped she stayed for the Beer Pong after all.

* * * * *

I felt a little odd, sitting in the **CT Hall cluster** in my jacket and tie, but going back to my own room was out of the question—the Pundits were probably already waiting for me—and there was something I had to check.

The clue had said "Act II, scene iii, line 20." I found a copy of *Macbeth* online and found the passage:

Anon anon, I pray you,
remember the Porter.

Remember the Porter? There'd been a time when wealthy students used to come to Yale with servants . . . But no, it had to be connected to the quote about the poisoned chalice. I found myself wishing that Nina was with me to help out.

CT Hall cluster: A computer cluster is a room filled with Macs and PCs that anyone with a Yale ID can use. Most people just stop by for five minutes to check email or to print something out (seven cents a page). But some find the austere setting helps them work faster, even if it's only so they can go home sooner.

CHAPTER TWELVE | 114

Faced with a difficult problem, I did what I always did: checked my email. There was nothing new, just another invitation to that **cast party** up on Dwight Street... Suddenly it hit me.

"Stupid!" I shouted, drawing a dirty look from the one poor soul typing a paper in the far corner.

The **Commencement Musical** last spring had been the third Dramat show I'd worked on, and after we finished taking down the set, **I'd been initiated** into the group by drinking a shot of Jack Daniels from a ceremonial cup. Initiations, cups, whiskey... all standard Yale stuff. Except this particular cup was called the **Porter Chalice**.

I didn't even bother to read the email. I just noted the address, logged out, and bolted up the stairs. I hadn't been in the show, of course, but I could still stop by and tell them what a great job I assumed they did. With any luck, the Chalice would be there. I pulled out my cell phone and dialed Nina. She didn't pick up—probably she wasn't talking to me right now. I hoped that she'd at least listen to the message. "Nina!" I gasped, slightly out of breath and too excited to compose myself. "I figured out the next clue! *Macbeth*! Scene wrong! Dramat party on Dwight Street! No time! Hurry!" I hung up and sprinted for the High Street gate, hoping I wasn't overdressed for the party.

---

cast party: You remember, don't you? From Chapter One! I bet you didn't think that was coming back.

Commencement Musical: Every year, the Dramat puts on a musical the weekend before commencement. Note to musicians: your friends in the Dramat will try to get you to play in the pit for this. Don't. Just don't.

I'd been initiated: Students are inducted into the Dramat after they work on three productions. However, you're kicked out if you don't go (or send a proxy) to the biannual Dramat elections. Judging by how hard most members try to get people to serve as their proxies, the elections must be a living hell.

Porter Chalice: This cup was indeed once owned by Cole Porter, given to him by his father after the premiere of a show. It was then stolen by one of his friends and given to the Dramat.

CHAPTER
Thirteen

"So I'm giving the big monologue at the beginning," said my friend Peter Fenzel, "and I get to this line 'Shorty Hawkins is gettin' ready to flag the five forty-five for Boston.' And there's supposed to be a train whistle. So I'm standing there, calmly, waiting for it . . ."

I smiled and nodded, but all I was thinking was, *Don't look down.*

In retrospect, I should have read the email about the cast party. I was in fact overdressed, as was everyone else when they showed up. It was a **naked party**.

When I'd arrived and seen a few dozen nude bodies making small talk, I had considered turning back—but I'd jogged all the way up there, and besides, some of the people in there were in a lot worse shape than I was. I threw my clothes in the pile with everyone else's and headed in.

"So," I asked Pete. "How's that play you're working on?" I was glad to be talking to him—

naked party:
A strange Yale tradition in which students show up at someone's off-campus apartment, strip down, and exchange polite conversation while sipping cocktails. Rule #1: Don't get excited. Rule #2: No, seriously, don't get excited. Rule #3: All right, go sit in the corner until you're fit for human company again. Live bands (also naked) have been known to play at these things, but you might want to adopt a more restrained style of dancing. Naked parties are by invitation only, and getting an invite lends you a certain cache, even if you don't go.

both because he was a good friend that I hadn't seen for a while and because he had cheated a little on his nudity and was wearing a strategically draped gray and red Berkeley scarf from J. Press.

"I'm going to apply for **Sudler funding** next semester," he said. "I'll let you know when it happens!"

He pushed past me toward the bar. I took a quick step backward to keep my distance from him, which caused me to bump right into a girl I didn't know. "Sorry, sorry," I said. I felt distressingly uncertain of what to do with my hands. I just bobbed to Madonna on the stereo.

Finally, the Dramat president walked into the room holding a **silver cup**. "Here it is, ladies and gentlemen. Members only, step right up and wet your . . . *whistles*." This got a big laugh.

"I said I was sorry!" cried the girl who had evidently been running the sound board.

I sighed in relief. Finally, I could take a quick look at the chalice and get my clothes back on. I started to thread my way across the room, careful to maintain at least a foot of buffer. Suddenly I felt a hand on my shoulder and jumped.

"Whoa, Miles! Easy there!"

You've got to be kidding me, I thought.

I turned and smiled at Perfect Paul. "Hey Paul! I didn't know you were in the Dramat."

"Got in last month, after I directed that musical version of *Equus* in the **OBT**. See, that's why we've

---

Sudler funding: The Sudler Fund gives out grants of up to $1,200 for student art. They're pretty democratic about it: your project could be a play, a film, a sculpture made out of chocolate, or a fashion show (which actually happened in 2005). The fund is distributed through the Masters' offices—for best results, mention a few other people in your college who want to be involved, so it'll look like a local affair.

silver cup: Actually, the chalice only comes out for the induction of new members. Shhh.

OBT: The Off-Broadway Theater. Located behind Toad's, this highly versatile space is the premiere location for non-dramat undergrad productions.

got to go out to lunch more often!" Jeez, he even had perfectly groomed chest hair.

Wait a sec, I thought. *If Paul's here, then that means . . .*

"Hi Miles," said a cool voice from behind me. I wheeled, somehow found myself looking right at Nina's chest, and almost dropped my glass of **Dubra** and cranberry juice. I quickly planted my eyes on her forehead and then realized I'd forgotten to say anything.

"Hi Nina. Good to see you." Then I worried that this would be perceived as an inappropriate innuendo. "You look good," I added. *Oh God, that was way worse.*

"Can I talk to you for a second?" she said, grabbing me by the arm and leading me away.

"Whoa!" said Paul good-naturedly. "Talking to my naked girlfriend! If I were the jealous type, you'd have some explaining to do!" But of course he wasn't the jealous type. The jerk.

I expected her to be mad, but for some reason she just looked guilty, which actually made me feel worse. "This is awkward," said Nina when we had reached a quiet corner. "I'll make up an excuse and leave."

"What do you mean?"

She shifted her weight uncomfortably. I tried not to pay attention to anything else that shifted. "I just don't really feel like we should be at this particular type of party together," she said. "I'm just here

> **Dubra:** A staple of college parties the nation over, Dubra is a brand of vodka that comes in plastic bottles and tastes like the pain of the Russian people. You'll get to know its cousin, Popov, too.

because Paul asked me to come, and I don't want to chase you away from your friends . . ."

"Nina, you don't understand! The next clue's here! It's the Porter Chalice—that cup he's passing around!"

Her eyes widened. "Seriously?"

"I tried to call you on the way over, but I guess you don't have your cell phone on you. For obvious reasons."

She stepped back and gave me an appraising look. "And I was so convinced that you didn't care about finding the Opal . . . "

I shrugged, trying to seem nonchalant.

"Does anyone else want to shake hands with Jack?" called the Dramat president.

"Well, what are you waiting for!" she said. Her eyes were shining with that old light again. Normally I would have been too shy to meet her gaze, but the way she was dressed, I was scared to look anywhere else.

* * * * *

Minutes later, I made my excuses and headed out. Nina was already waiting for me on **Dwight Street**. "That was quick. What did you tell Paul?" I asked.

"Oh, standard stuff. I wasn't comfortable with the nudity, my poor innocent freshman liver couldn't handle the Kamikaze shots I was drinking. Now he probably won't tell me about these parties anymore,"

Dwight Street:
A typical off-campus housing tradeoff. The place may be very nice, but you're going to need a bicycle.

Why not just drive? Well, if you want to have a car on campus, your cheapest option is to get a permit for the Pierson-Sage Yale lot. Unfortunately, your cheapest option is more than $600 a year. Or you can try your luck at keeping your car on the streets, but you'll have to move it everyday. The bottom line is not many students find it worth it to keep a car around.

she said with an annoyed shrug. "But screw him; what was the clue?"

"Inside the handle of the TD bell."

"Are you *sure*?"

"Positive."

"How do you know?"

"The writing at the bottom of the cup said, 'Look inside the handle of the TD bell.' I guess the Pundits figured you'd be pretty drunk when you read that, so they kept it simple."

"The who?" I quickly filled her in on what I'd been up to since we'd parted outside of Stiles. She politely swallowed her laughter when I explained how Jessica had cowed me with a fake gun.

"Well, that explains why you wore a suit to a naked party," she said, when I was finished. "You're confident that they had nothing to do with Quinlan getting . . . you know . . . falling?"

"I doubt they could organize anything that doesn't somehow involve whoopee cushions. I plan to keep my eyes open, though."

"Okay. I'll trust your judgement." She smiled at me, and then she frowned again.

"What now?"

"The TD bell. Everyone in TD worships that thing. No way they'll let us disassemble it."

The **minibus** pulled up, and we climbed in. "Old Campus," Nina told the driver. We sat in silence, mulling it over.

"You know," I mused, "Gary's in TD."

minibus: The minibuses run set routes from 6 P.M. to 1 A.M. After that they can be summoned to pick you up anywhere and take you to the destination of your choice. Try to resist calling the driver "Jeeves" as you order him around.

She looked skeptical. "You want to bring Captain Conspicuous back on board?"

"Okay, he goes a little overboard sometimes, but we can trust him," I assured her. "To be involved with this, he'd take a vow of silence."

There was a doubtful pause. "If I get murdered because of him," she said, "I'm blaming you."

"Fair enough."

The bus pulled to a stop at Phelps Gate. As Nina climbed off, she paused and turned to me again. "Miles, I'm sorry. I shouldn't have accused you of not caring about the hunt. I would never have gotten anywhere without you."

"So we're still partners?"

"Still."

"Good. Well, let's both get some sleep. I'll let you know what the plan is once I've talked to Gary."

The driver reached for the lever to close the door, but Nina suddenly stuck her head back into the bus. "Miles, where are you going to sleep? You can't go home; the Pundits will Tase you."

"Uh," I said uncertainly.

"My roommate has a boyfriend with a single, so she's never home . . ."

"No no, I'll stay with the Puh." As long as I was about to ask him for one giant favor, it might as well be two. "Besides," I said with forced levity, "Paul will get out of that party soon enough, and you don't want that empty dorm room to go to waste, right?"

"I guess not," she said, blushing slightly. For a minute, she seemed about to say something else, but then she stepped back.

CHAPTER THIRTEEN

The visibly annoyed bus driver seized the opportunity to shut the door. I watched her watch me pull away.

"Where to?" the driver asked.

"TD," I told him. I got out my phone and called Gary. He had picked a high number at last year's **housing draw**, so he'd ended up in a cramped double on the fourth floor. But it would have to do.

"WOOOOOOOO!" he screamed, barely audible over the blaring techno.

"Gary? Where the hell are you?"

"Toad's! I'm on the booty **cam**!"

"Well then do everyone there a favor, and step outside so I can talk to you!" I heard movement on the other end, and the crowd noise and music grew quieter.

"Listen," I said. "I need your help. I'm in big trouble—I'm caught up in something that I can't even begin to explain, and I need you to help me at the Game tomorrow. But you're going to have to betray all your highest principles." Gary took a deep breath. "I can make it worth your while!" I said quickly.

"How?"

"I will tell you something about Yale that you don't know."

There was a long pause. "Then I'm in," he said.

housing draw: Housing draw is the process by which the rooms in the residential colleges are assigned to students for the following year. In most cases this means getting a group of friends together to go for a particular suite. But since suites in a single college can have anywhere between two and eight people, your carefully assembled group may have to quickly reorganize in a matter of minutes if things don't go your way. It's different for every college, but everyone agrees that it's painful and confusing.

cam: A giant screen over the dance floor projects video of the most impressive and hardest working booties in the joint. For those fortunate enough to have their badonkadonks projected Kong-sized for all of New Haven to see, the thrill is greater than graduating summa cum laude.

Party Time
Species of Yale Party

College parties are generally deemed successful to the extent that they resemble dance clubs: an ideal party would have a sound system with a ridiculous subwoofer, a full bar, and a fog machine. Oddly enough, recent graduates report that nightclubs are successful to the extent that they resemble college parties: ideally, you wouldn't have to pay for booze, everyone you know would be there, and no one older than thirty would show up. Aside from the aforementioned Naked Party, here are some of the typical Yale parties you will make a fool of yourself at during your time at the school.

Basic Dorm Parties

You'll send out a bulk email, shove the coffee table into your room, and hook up someone's iPod to the stereo. The alcohol consists of a few plastic bottles of Dubra with OJ to mix, some Mike's Hard Lemonade for the ladies, and maybe a keg in the shower if you're feeling ambitious. At first, only your friends will show up, then other people in the college, and by the end of the night guys you've never seen will be passed out on your bed. Note: if there's a party anywhere in your entryway, try to barricade your bathroom. Otherwise, plan not to go in there for a couple days.

Organization Parties

These will be held in the dorm room of someone in the organization. They're not really so different from any other dorm party except the inside jokes and gossip will scare away anyone who's not part of the group. If you're in the organization, it's fun because all your friends are there. But it's dangerous because all your friends are drunk and suddenly one of them looks kind of hot, and before you know it you're a Yale stereotype. Many of these parties are thrown within the first week or two of school to recruit the impressionable froshlings.

Party Suite Parties

The Cottage, Bookworld, the JE Sextet . . . addresses that are legend at Yale. These suites are ideally laid out for entertaining, and over the years it's become tradition that the inhabitants be stalwart party animals. In some cases the residents are elected by members of the college. And some even receive college funds to throw their bacchanals. Your local party suite is a good place to start out the night, meeting up with friends before heading to DKE or Toad's.

Wine and Cheese Parties

Any early evening soiree. The wine? In big boxes, served in red plastic cups. The cheese? Whatever was in the deli counter at Gourmet Heaven, or the kind you spray from a can. But by God, sir, we are Yalies! And we shall have our *Great Gatsby* playtime. Good day, sir!

Frat Parties

The beer flows like water and tastes like water. The frat party is exactly like the dorm party times two. You're twice as likely to run into someone you know. You're twice as likely to lose the people you came with. You're twice as likely to get served a drink. You're going to wait twice as long to get it. They're a fun time, though—just the feeling of being out off campus at somebody's house is exciting in a limited way, and besides, the dorm parties sometimes get shut down by zealous college Masters. The fraternities are their own masters—but then again, the frat parties are sometimes shut down by the police.

Themed Parties

Yalies are creative and tend to get excited over gimmicks. Themes run from minimal (SAE's Night of 1000 Jell-O Shots) to the elaborate (the D-port Cottage Porn Party, where you go dressed as your favorite porn character and do shots out of a paper-mache . . . uh, you get the idea).

Official Parties

The college dining halls will occasionally turn into giant dance floors. No booze to be had here, but the music is better, the floors aren't a sticky mess, and you can always pre- (and post-) party somewhere else. They range from the eighties-themed Safety Dance to the formal Winter Ball. These parties have become less common as Yale renovates the colleges and the Masters start thinking twice about the entire student body trampling their nice new carpets.

CHAPTER

Fourteen

The next morning, as I walked down the tunnel of the **Yale Bowl**, "10,000 Men of Harvard" sputtered to a close and the PA crackled to life. "Good afternoon ladies and gentlemen," said a crisp baritone. "Will the owner of a gray Lexus, license plate STK478, please report to the press box. Your car has been vomited upon by THE MEMBERS OF . . ."

Twenty thousand Yalies replied, "THE YALE . . . PRECISION . . . MARCHING . . . BAND!"

The Harvard band wears spotless black pants and maroon jackets neatly buttoned over polka-dotted ties—your choice of knot. **The Yale Precision Marching Band** wears white pants from the local Salvation Army, often with several years' worth of grass and ketchup stains on them, and a variety of T-shirts covered with blue

Yale Bowl: Built in 1914, it originally held up to 80,000 people, making it the largest coliseum since Rome's. The place was packed every weekend; pretty amazing considering the whole student body was only a few thousand. The benches haven't been completely filled in decades—Ivy league football ain't what it used to be. Nevertheless, Yalies generally love the Bowl, which oozes character even more than the rest of the campus.

The Yale Precision Marching Band: The members of the Yale Precision Marching Band don't really march. At all. Instead, they run haphazardly into place, with a minimum of precision. Recent halftime shows have included Dubya's nose snorting a giant line of cocaine, a gun control sketch that involved a bloody shootout between Elmo and Big Bird, and a highly condensed performance of *Oedipus Rex*, during which the band spelled "MILF" and played Alanis Morissette's "Ironic."

blazers decorated with enough buttons to earn a Friday's waitress Employee of the Month. So on the whole, impersonating a Harvard band member is a lot harder, but luckily a friend who had one of them crashing in his common room the night before had been kind enough to swipe her blazer.

I stepped out of the tunnel into the **hahvahd** student section and took a moment to enjoy the view. Across the stadium, the Yale fans were on their feet, a teeming mass of blue punctuated with waving residential college flags. A few hearty souls had jumped the gun on the Saybrook Strip and were dancing happily in their underwear. Even though I was in enemy territory, about to do something very stupid, I smiled. It was the Game.

The halftime show was a loose reenactment of WWI. A cardboard squadron of blue Yale biplanes dogfought with the Crimson Baron's flying circus, while a cardboard tank rolled over a few "Harvard students" (actually red-clad Yalies doing their best to look like idiots). The band spelled "V-H DAY" on the field and played "London Calling."

I made my way down the steps to the field. The security guard took one look at my blazer and waved me onto the sideline, even though the rest of the Harvard band was filing back into the stands. I stood by a goalpost until the YPMB kicked into **"Down the Field"** and scrambled into the traditional "ELI YALE" formation, three of their sousaphones spouting smoke and flames (presumably on purpose).

---

hahvahd: If you're full of Yale spirit (and at the Game, who isn't?) then Yale's archrival is *never* "Harvard." It's "hahvahd": thick Boston accent, lower case *h*. Particularly jingoistic Yalies simply refer to it as "that school up north," or "Cambridge Community College."

"Down the Field": Yale has an embarrassment of fight song riches. "Boola Boola" was swiped by Oklahoma and became "Boomer Sooner." "Bulldog" and "Bingo" are both early Cole Porter tunes. And "Down the Field" was ranked the number four fight song of all time in the book *College Fight Songs: An Annotated Anthology*. Don't graduate without hearing the Glee Club perform its fight song medley.

CHAPTER FOURTEEN

Suddenly, the Yale crowd's cheering surged as the Puh ran onto the field, carrying the TD flag with one hand and ringing the bell with the other. Luckily for me, when I'd told him what had been happening over the past couple of days he was too excited to be upset that I'd kept him in the dark. He had gotten pretty upset when I explained my plan—but I'd managed to talk him into it eventually. "Good old Puh," I said softly.

Pulling my crimson scarf around my face, I ran toward him. The Puh pretended not to notice me. I heard the whole TD student section crying in sudden alarm as I pushed the Puh from behind, snatched the bell, and headed for the nearest exit. "You owe me one, Bowman!" he screamed at me as I sprinted away.

For a moment it looked like a security guard was going to grab me, but I'd obviously played a lot more **intramural football** than he had—a simple fake to the right and spin to the left and I was in the tunnel, sprinting toward freedom. The YPMB was just finishing up, and I couldn't help but sing along with them in a sudden burst of euphoria. "Harvard's team may fight till the end BUT YALE . . . WILL . . . WIN!"

Outside of the Bowl, the **tailgates** perfumed the air with grill smoke and Milwaukee's Best, but also with lobster tails and champagne. After all, this was the Game, the last place on earth where a raccoon skin coat is an acceptable fashion choice. I quickly

intramural football: The colleges play each other in dozens of sports, from table tennis to ice hockey. At the end of the year, the college with the most points overall is awarded the coveted Tyng Cup (and free T-shirts!). There is also a Davie Cup, awarded to the college with the most participation, but this cup is for losers. Although students are randomly assigned to their colleges—and therefore they all should be equally gifted athletically—there are certain ones that are traditional powerhouses and others that can barely drag themselves out to the field. Must be something in the pipes.

tailgates: The colleges and fraternities all rent U-Hauls, park them in a row over on the practice fields, and create a gauntlet of barbeques. Before the Game (and well into the first half), it seems like the entire student body and a lot of recent alumni are making the rounds, screaming to be heard over a dozen stereos, ankle deep in discarded cups.

stripped off the blazer, wrapped the bell inside it, and put it behind a garbage can. Out of the corner of my eye, I could see Nina strolling in to collect it. Without looking back, I hurried to the men's room and waited in a stall for five minutes. I emerged wearing a Yale T-shirt and blue face paint.

"Safety school!" said a crimson-clad girl.

"School on **Monday**," I retorted, glancing around nervously for possible pursuers. No one was rushing at me. Walking back to the Yale student section, I breathed a sigh of relief. Right now, half of TD was probably busy beating up the Harvard Marching Band. I'd anonymously return the bell after we got the clue out of the handle that night, and no one would be the wiser.

That's when a security guard tapped me on the shoulder.

"Excuse me," he said, none too friendly. "I'm going to have to ask you to come with me."

Monday: Yale students leave the Game and head home for Thanksgiving break. Harvard students somehow have to recover and attend two more days of class. That alone is reason enough not to go there.

Go Back to the Yahd

Why Yale Is Better Than Harvard

You knew this list was coming. The reasons are numerous.

1. Spend a Saturday night at Yale, then spend a Saturday night at Harvard. You won't even have to read the rest of the list.

2. Harvard cares more about its grad schools than about undergraduate education. Its student-to-faculty ratio is higher than Yale's, and even with its mighty endowment, Harvard ranks *tenth* in per-student spending. (Yale ranks second.)

3. Harvard's academic schedule places your exams immediately after holiday break, thus making you skip Christmas to study. Bunch of Scrooges.

4. In 2005, three Elis won Rhodes Scholarships. Harvard? None. Looks like that extra studying really paid off.

5. From the Harvard *Crimson*: "Few Harvard students are content to take part in extracurriculars for their own sakes; involvement is almost always contingent upon rising up the ranks to a leadership position."

6. A secret memo obtained by the *Boston Globe* reveals that when the students of thirty-one top schools were surveyed, Harvard ranked a lowly twenty-sixth in student satisfaction. "I think we have to concede that we are letting our students down," said Lawrence Buell, the former dean of undergraduate education.

7. Harvard has no theater department.

8. In 2004, desperate to improve its students' nonexistent social lives, Harvard hired a recent graduate as "special assistant to the dean for social programming," quickly dubbed the "Fun Czar." It gets better. A few months later, over fifty Harvard students had to be treated for alcohol poisoning after the Game. "It was a disgrace," said Captain William Evans of the Boston Police. "I had officers come up to me and say they'd never seen an event so embarrassing." Party on, Cantabs. Party on.

9. In February 2006, President Larry Summers was forced to resign by his disgruntled faculty. His term had lasted only five years. Harvard law professor William Stuntz complained in an article for *The New Republic* that: "Harvard is . . . rich, bureaucratic, and confident, a deadly combination. . . . From now on, the decline will likely be steep."

10. In 2001, the *Boston Globe* reported that 91 percent of Harvard students graduated with honors. About half of all grades issued were As.

11. Harvard dean of admissions William Fitzsimmon: "You probably aren't going to get calls every day in your room asking you do you want to come out to play or go to lunch. It's not the way Harvard works."

12. According to the National Institutes of Health, in 2002, 69 percent of Harvard students felt exhausted up to ten times during the year, 65 percent felt overwhelmed by all they had to do, and 48 percent felt things were hopeless. Jeez, let's all go up there and hug them.

CHAPTER
Fifteen

When I arrived at **Coxe Cage**, most people were hastily gulping down their cider and hot chocolate while bundling up to get back to the Bowl. The security guard led me to the back of the massive building, where a few tables were roped off with a sign that said "Welcome Back Alumni." The only people still there were a few old geezers in tweed, either too feeble to be outdoors or too senile to know that the game was halfway over already.

Dean Sheely was sitting at a table in the corner, alone save for a large plate of pasta salad. I sat down next to him, and the security guard wandered off toward the buffet himself.

"The greatest thing about this university," Sheely said, "is the catering. Perhaps I would have retired long ago were it not for the never-ending array of cheese platters and spinach puffs. Do you know that Louis XIV once had three chefs abducted from the harem of the Ottoman Sultan Ahmed II and chained to the stove at Versailles?"

Coxe Cage: A giant indoor track facility right next to the Bowl. The Cage's 26,000-square-foot skylight is one of the largest in the world. During the Game, Coxe Cage hosts a giant "indoor tailgate." Having a warm place to retreat to is nice indeed, but since entry costs twenty dollars and the event is decidedly alcohol-free, it's more of an alumni thing.

CHAPTER FIFTEEN | 134

"We've already met," I fumed, "so you can spare me your traditional spiel."

"Very well." He reached out and touched my forehead, then held up his index finger, looking at the blue stain as if it were something nasty he had stepped in. "To business. Tell me, Mr. Bowman, why did you steal the TD bell?"

There wasn't much sense in playing dumb. But if I played cocky and got him angry at me, I could probably keep Nina and Gary out of it. "I guess deep down I always wanted to be in **JE**," I said.

"I will assume that you have made some sort of undergrad witticism. Did I not inform you that the halls of ExCom are littered with the desiccated carcasses of my antagonists?"

I was sick of being bullied. "It was a stupid prank and I apologize," I said calmly. "But you can't Ex-Com me for a prank."

"To be sure, to be sure." He leaned back in his chair enough to make it creak. "But I don't believe either you or Miss Lennox is authorized to enter Harkness Tower." I turned white. "And certainly your recent activities at the Beinecke are sufficient to see you cast out on your ear."

I blinked at him. Harkness I understood all too well, but the Beinecke? I hadn't been there since I toured the university during **Bulldog Days**. Unless . . .

"These are serious infractions," he continued. "But if you hand over the TD bell to me, posthaste,

---

JE: JE and TD have a rivalry that goes way back. In 1948, TD even "kidnapped" A. Whitney Griswold, one of JE's fellows. (He was released and went on to become president of the university.)

Bulldog Days: A couple days in April, during which the newly admitted pre-frosh are invited to campus. A few are still trying to decide if Yale is for them, but many are already committed, and Bulldog Days is just a chance to start meeting their new Facebook friends.

I may be able to convince some of the committee's members to look leniently upon your case."

"Dean Sheely," I said quietly. "There *is* something I didn't tell you the last time we met."

He raised an eyebrow.

"When I went to see Professor Quinlan that afternoon, I brought him a book. I didn't think it was important at the time."

"Your judgment was poor," he snapped. "What was this book called?"

"*The Philogyny.*"

"I see. And do you have any idea why Professor Quinlan would have cared about a jokebook?"

"Interesting," I said, "that you know it's a jokebook."

He frowned at me. "I'm an educated man, Mr. Bowman. Of course I know what *The Philogelos* is!"

"Except I didn't say that." I was grinning now, and Sheely seemed frozen. "I said 'philogyny.' It means 'a fondness for women.' From the Greek, *philos*, meaning 'loving, dear,' and *gyne*, meaning 'woman, or wife.'"

Thank you **SAT prep courses**, I thought.

His mouth worked furiously.

"Let me guess," I went on, "you spent the last two days trying to figure out a way to get at the Gutenberg Bible?"

From his expression of surprised rage, it was obvious that he had.

SAT prep courses: As an alternative, why not consider using a SparkNotes book to help you prepare? We have several guides to the SAT. (It's our book. We can plug all we like. Just try to stop us.)

"God, and you had me leave the clue under Marlowe?" I laughed. "When you're teaching a class on film noir? Not only is that careless, it displays a lack of creativity."

"I am not amused by your groundless conspiracy theories, Mr. Bowman."

"I should say that you wouldn't be! You keep talking about the deep friendship between you and Professor Quinlan. Were you Pundits together?"

"Hogwash," he said, agitated. "Jeremiah and I met when we were in the **Yale Concert Band**. We . . ."

"You knew about the book, Sheely," I interrupted him. "There's only one group of people who know that *The Philogelos* is important."

He looked distinctly ill. Finally, he narrowed his eyes at me. "Very well, Mr. Bowman. I was a Pundit with my dear friend Jeremiah. It was his lifelong dream to find the Eli Opal—a dream I have no intention of letting you usurp."

"So you stole my library books?" I exclaimed. "Dean Sheely, did you know that at the library of Alexandria, if one scholar stole scrolls from another, the offender was executed by means of a million paper cuts?"

"Thankfully," he growled, "we no longer live in those benighted times."

"That was a lie," I told him coolly. Then I frowned. "It wasn't just bad luck that I got caught at the Bowl, was it? You couldn't get to the next clue,

> **Yale Concert Band:** The Yale Concert Band plays everything from world premiere compositions to Sousa marches. Shockingly, many members of the Yale Precision Marching Band are talented enough to be a part of both organizations.

so you had me watched, hoping I'd lead you to it. That security guard was just waiting until he saw me do something unusual."

"All your speculations are beside the point," he said scornfully. "You are the one who has been caught committing wrongdoing, not I. Now give me the bell, and perhaps you will be allowed to finish out your sophomore year."

"As a Yale dean," I said quietly, "you have access to Harkness Tower. Did you kill Quinlan?"

He executed another color change, this time to purple. "You go too far. No one killed him. He slipped."

I shook my head. "Nina got a threatening email right after—"

"Has it ever occurred to you," he sneered, "that she may have sent it to herself? And you gave her the bell, didn't you? Fool. She's probably long gone . . ."

"Dean Sheely?" said a soft voice. Nina walked up and placed the bell on the desk. "I just want you to know that the prank was entirely my idea. In fact, Miles believed that the students of TD were in on it, and this was just a kickoff for the freshman scavenger hunt. I take full responsibility."

Sheely stared at her for a moment, then calmly accepted the bell, which he placed on the table in front of him. "Very well," he said, his voice full of contempt. "You leave me little choice but to recommend to ExCom that you both be expelled."

"What?" shouted Nina.

"But you promised not to if I gave you the bell!" I protested.

"Yes, I lied," he said, taking a bite of a cookie. "It is, as you said, my traditional spiel."

There was a long, painful pause. "Can I at least have my library books back?" I asked.

"No."

Yale Myths Debunked

Yale Myths, or "Lies My Tour Guide Told Me"

Did you like Sheely's lie? Here, then! Have some more!

The CIA wanted the Nathan Hale statue that stands on Old Campus for itself, as he is widely considered to be the nation's first spy. Yale refused. So one night, CIA agents snuck onto the Old Campus and tried to steal it, only to be discovered and chased away by the freshman class. (A replica of the statue does stand outside the agency's headquarters in Langley, but they never tried to abscond with the original.)

When Cornelius Vanderbilt gave the money for a freshman dorm on the Old Campus in 1899, he did so with one stipulation: that whenever a Vanderbilt came to Yale, he would get to live there. This didn't happen until 1969, at which point young Vanderbilt got to be the only man in a dorm of 300 women. (Not true, but it would make a great movie. Get on that.)

The central column of books in the Beinecke Library (built during the Cold War) is designed to drop down into the ground in the event of a nuclear war. (Actually, the water table beneath Beneicke is high enough to make this plan impossible.)

Harkness Tower was once the tallest freestanding stone structure in the world. But builders tossed acid on it to make it look older and mistakenly weakened it to the point where it needed to be reinforced. (It *was* doused in acid, but it didn't need to be reinforced until 1981.)

After residential college architect James Gambel Rogers died, his son took over the project. Rogers Jr. was not a fan of Gothic architecture and decided to finish the remaining colleges in the Georgian style, explaining why D-port is split between both styles. (The elder Rogers lived until 1947, way after the colleges were done.)

In the 1930s, Mrs. Payne Whitney gave the school a ton of money for a church. What Yale really needed was a gym, so the administrators had the architects make Payne Whitney look like a cathedral from the outside so the feeble old woman could be driven past it. (C'mon, you think this would actually work?)

CHAPTER
Sixteen

When I felt depressed, I always went to **Woolsey Hall**. The thousands of empty wooden seats made the perfect surroundings for a good sulk. If I really wanted to wallow, I'd climb up to the balcony and sit in the **Taft chair**, which made me feel especially small.

"He can't really get us expelled just for taking the bell, can he?" asked Nina, sitting next to me. Her voice sounded tiny in the massive space.

"We'll see, I guess," I said. Outside, we could hear a happy crowd of students walking by, bellowing "**Bright College Years**" at the top of their lungs. With Yale having won its first Game in recent memory, everyone who hadn't already caught a flight was hurrying out to celebrate (at least a little, before exhaustion set in). All the good cheer only made us feel worse.

Woolsey Hall: The university's main auditorium. One of your earliest Yale memories will be sitting with the entire freshman class to hear the dean give a speech, looking over the hundreds of faces of your new classmates, and wondering how many of these people you will someday have sex with. Maybe that's just us, actually.

Taft chair: William Howard Taft, Yale alum, president of the United States, chief justice of the Supreme Court, and a very fat tub of lard, had a special seat installed at the front of the first balcony to accommodate his, um, ass. Go early to a symphony concert and sit in it, pretending to twirl your mustache and break up trusts. It's awesome.

"Bright College Years:" Yale's alma mater. Penned in 1881, it unfortunately shares the tune of "*Die Wacht am Rhein*," which became a favorite anthem of the Nazis. On the last line of BCY, ("For God, for Country, and for Yale"), students traditionally wave their handkerchiefs in time with the music. That is, they used to wave their handkerchiefs, when people still carried handkerchiefs.

CHAPTER SIXTEEN | 142

organ: The Newberry Memorial Organ (one of the ten largest in the world) is regarded by organ aficionados to be one of the great instruments on the American continent. Even if you're not particularly musical, you can appreciate what an amazing racket the thing can make. Yale has an official organist on the payroll, who performs occasional concerts.

bathroom: The upside of sharing a bathroom between multiple suites is that the university cleans it . . . and this is a fantastic trade-off. The Yale bathrooms that students have to clean themselves quickly become completely unfit for man or beast. People have been known to stay in bad relationships just to have a place to shower besides their horrible bathroom. Most of these self-service bathrooms are on the Old Campus—Durfee, Farnum, and the top level of Vanderbilt have them—but there are parts of the residential colleges where they turn up too.

Nina and I stared at the **organ** in the distance, the corners of the room gradually disappearing into the shadows.

"Thanks again for rescuing me," I told her.

"Actually, you should thank Paul. He saw you being dragged over there."

"What was he doing outside of the Bowl?"

"Teaching disadvantaged children to skip rope."

I admit that I called him an extremely rude, unprintable name here.

"I kid," she said. "I kid. He was coming back from the bathroom."

That made me feel better. Still, I wasn't going to thank him.

"You think we're *really* going to be expelled?" she asked me nervously, for like the eighth time.

I nodded bleakly. "And I was looking forward to going to Myrtle Beach my senior year."

"And I was looking forward to not having to clean my own **bathroom** as a sophomore." We both let out a long, sad sigh.

"Well, instead we can both look forward to careers cleaning other people's bathrooms," I said. "Or sorting slides at the **Center for British Art**. If we're lucky."

"C'mon Miles," she said with a forced smile. "Don't look so *blue*."

"Am I still wearing the face paint?" I said.

"Yeah."

"Funny." But neither of us laughed.

My phone buzzed again. I had seventeen voice mail messages, all from Gary. The poor guy was probably desperate to know what the clue was. I didn't have the heart to tell him the bad news yet.

"Well," Nina said, trying to muster a little cheerfulness, "ExCom probably won't convene until after finals. So we can keep trying to find the Opal. For a little while, at least."

The cavernous room seemed painfully quiet. Hard to believe I'd enjoyed the **Halloween Show** there only weeks ago.

I shook my head. "Nina, Sheely's an ex-Pundit. He knows all about the Opal. He knew I was going after it and had me followed."

Her gasp echoed for five seconds. "And now he has the clue! I'm so stupid!" she groaned.

"It's okay," I said. "You couldn't have known. But he'll never let us get our hands on the bell again."

I stared at the painted figures on the gilded ceiling, barely visible in the twilight.

"Except," she said, with a hint of her old swagger, "we don't need to get our hands on it."

I looked at her. "What are you talking about?"

Center for British Art: In addition to the amazing, free-to-students Art Gallery—the best kept secret on the Yale campus, by the way—Yale also has the Center for British Art, which has the largest collection of British art outside of England. Everybody get in line for "The Worlds of Francis Wheatley"! Oh, wait, there is no line.

Halloween Show: The Yale Symphony Orchestra packs Woolsey every year for its annual Halloween Show, at which they screen an original silent movie and provide a live score, which usually involves a rock band at some point. Worth seeing, if only for the disturbingly phallic costumes and the cameos by administrators.

She grinned inscrutably and passed me a badly crumpled piece of paper.

"What's this?" I said. "A page from one of the Game programs?"

"Other side," she said.

I flipped it over. There was a message written in Nina's neat handwriting:

Aha Pundit! You are too late! I, Benjamin Silliman, have regained the gem!

My eyes widened. "Is this—"

"I unscrewed the handle and copied it down before I went to Coxe Cage to find you," she beamed. "I wasn't sure when we'd have another opportunity."

We were already facing expulsion. The part of me smart enough to get into Yale said I should just head to **Rudy's** and forget about gems altogether. But when Nina was grinning like that, the smart part of me didn't call the shots.

"When do you leave campus?" I asked.

"Tomorrow morning."

"Good, I'm staying the night too. Okay, so I'm assuming that you put the clue back in the bell?"

"I thought future generations might want to take a crack at it," she protested. "I didn't know the Dean was evil!"

"Don't beat yourself up about it. We'll just have to find the Opal before Sheely does," I said. The energy that had fueled me for the last few days was flowing back. "So what does the clue mean?"

Rudy's: Yale's dive bar of choice. It's dark, crowded, and the bathroom graffiti is interesting enough for a dissertation. But the jukebox is well-stocked, the Belgian fries are great, and the carding policy is, um, spotty, at best. Rudy's is a lot like the legendary football player of the same name: small, humble, and rarely starts the night but always ready to step in when you need it.

CHAPTER SIXTEEN

She frowned. "Is it possible that it's not a clue? Maybe Silliman really got the gem back."

"Nah. The Pundits said all these clues are only thirty years old. Silliman's been dead for . . . well, a lot of years."

We sat in thought, feeling the seconds slip away.

"He was buried around here, wasn't he?" Nina asked.

"Probably. Why?"

She nodded at me meaningfully.

"Oh no," I groaned. "They wouldn't have . . ."

"From everything you've told me, I think they probably would."

* * * * *

An hour later, Nina and I walked quickly along High Street, with the **Law School** on our left and the featureless marble of **Book and Snake** on our right. Ahead of us was **Grove Street Cemetery**, its stone gate the copper color of earth mixed with dried blood. In the darkness that fell early this time of year, floodlights illuminated the inscription on the lintel: "The Dead Shall Be Raised."

Law School: One of the best law schools in the country, but as far as you're concerned it's only important because you can "transfer" at the Law School dining hall, getting $6.65 worth of food for your swipe ($7.95 if it's dinner). If you know you're going to eat out at Louis' Lunch or something, instead of letting a prepaid meal go to waste, stop by the Law School and stock up on candy and Snapple.

Book and Snake: Said to be one of the more laid-back societies, Book and Snake was the first to admit minorities and women. Bob Woodward was a member, and we all know how much he hates secret conspiracies, so it can't be that bad.

Grove Street Cemetery: Created in 1797, Grove Street Cemetery is a national historic landmark, which is too bad for the Yale administration, which would probably love to move the bodies to Hamden and build something useful on that prime real estate. Famous people here include Eli Whitney, Noah Webster, and former commissioner of baseball A. Bartlett Giamatti.

shovel: Miles got this at Hull's Hardware. Only $19.56!

Swing Space: A very dormlike building curled in a fetal position between the gym and the cemetery. Swing Space houses the students of whichever college is being renovated that year. It's nice because you get a bathtub, a kitchenette, and air conditioning. It's not nice because you feel like you're living in a Days Inn, and you don't have a dining hall to call your own. Perhaps the saddest thing about it is that its official name on the maps is "New Residence Hall." And it ain't so new.

Zoo: The Computer Science Department's main undergraduate lab, a cluster of thirty-eight high-tech machines, running Linux, of course. Windows? They don't need your stinking Windows!

"You ain't kidding," I said, shifting my grip on the **shovel** hidden under my coat. Nina gave my free hand a squeeze, temporarily clearing my mind of all thoughts of grave-robbery.

We turned onto Ashmun Street and walked away from the traffic, past the **Swing Space**. Looking around once to make sure we had the street to ourselves, we scrambled over the wall and into the darkness of the cemetery. I was nervous, but as I was already facing expulsion, getting caught didn't seem like as much of an issue as it had been that morning.

We wandered among the ancient monuments until we found the Silliman family plot, behind a rusty iron fence. It was dominated by Benjamin Silliman's grave, which towered above me by two feet.

I looked at her. "Rock, paper, scissors?"

She nodded. I chose rock and lost.

Breaking the earth with my shovel, I had to fight the irrational fear that a skeletal hand would shoot up from the earth and seize me. I reminded myself that Benjamin Silliman was a man of science. If his vengeful corpse were magically reanimated, he would probably be too embarrassed about it to leave the coffin.

A foot down, my shovel produced a dull thunking sound that seemed painfully loud. I instinctively looked up at the **Zoo**, expecting to see a few nerds looking out at me curiously. But even the nerds were either flying home or off partying tonight.

My hands trembling a bit, I found the edges of what I'd hit and pried it out of the ground. It was a nondescript wooden box, about the size of a toaster. The latches were so caked in mud it took a minute to find them, but they worked. "This is it," Nina whispered. I opened the box.

There was no opal. There was a small wooden bird, with a message carefully carved into a wing: "You haffe fond the wilde goose!"

"What the hell . . ." said Nina.

The dismay I felt was so powerful that it was almost a physical sensation, similar to nausea. It was like when I found out that Santa Claus wasn't real, if Santa had been in the habit of handing out student loan payments and kidney-shaped swimming pools. *Oh well*, I thought darkly. *I suppose I can always go work for **McKinsey***.

"Thank you very much for undergoing the manual labor," said Sheely. We whirled to see him striding toward us like a ghost. "But I do not intend to stand by and watch you make off with what my dear friend spent his whole life pursuing. Give it here."

"Here's what Quinlan spent his whole life pursuing," I said bitterly, tossing the bird at his feet. "And you're welcome to it." He picked it up and stared at it for a long time.

"You planted this!" he barked.

McKinsey: The major consulting firms that recruit on campus are McKinsey & Company, Bain, and BCG. Not even the consultants themselves can really explain what it is that they do, but it seems that companies come to these firms to have twenty-three-year-olds with BAs in art history tell them how to improve their grocery store. Consulting is the kind of job that will demand long hours, and then demand you spend your meager free time participating in work-sponsored "team building" events, but if you're really looking to pay off those student loans fast and aren't overencumbered by a soul, feel free to sit through one of their five-hour-long job interviews.

I shook my head. "You were a Pundit. They love to fool people, right? Especially each other."

"My God," he whispered. He didn't move a muscle, but he suddenly looked a lot more at home among the tombstones. "The Opal doesn't exist? Just a prank? A foolish hippie prank! God, Jeremiah . . . it wasn't even real . . ." A cold wind rushed through the graveyard, tugging at Sheely's yellow, green, and red J. Press scarf.

Suddenly, something clicked for me.

"Quinlan died with his coat buttoned up," I said slowly, "and a scarf wrapped around his face. But it wasn't his scarf. It was a Silliman scarf. He was in Berkeley."

I let that sink in. Sheely stood frozen, a deer in the headlights. It was so quiet I thought I could hear the sound of a French horn floating out of the **Yale School of Music** three blocks away.

"You, however," I said quietly, "were in Silliman. Weren't you? If I went to J. Press, they would remember that you bought that scarf you're wearing now the morning after the professor died, wouldn't they?"

Sheely's rigid pomposity seemed to melt into the frigid air. "Yes," he said, his voice shaking. "I loaned him the scarf. Jeremiah . . . he was so excited that he'd left his warm clothes behind. He was so cold, so cold on the tower." He hardly seemed to be talking to us anymore. His eyes were focused on some point far away in the darkness.

Yale School of Music: Thanks to a recent anonymous donation, the School of Music is now tuition-free. Almost without fail, the sound of someone practicing is floating out of a window of this building at any and all hours.

"I would have shared!" he moaned. "But I wasn't walking off with nothing. That damn fool wanted to donate it to the Peabody!"

"So how did it happen?" Nina asked gently.

"It was an accident!" he shouted. "We were arguing, and then there was a scuffle . . . he fell and cracked his head on the steps. I didn't know what to do!"

"So you dragged your *dear* friend Jeremiah's body up to the top of the tower and tossed him off, trying to make it look like a suicide?"

He looked at her almost pleadingly, as if her forgiveness might fix everything. "What was I supposed to do?"

"Not that," she said icily.

"That's enough for me," I said. "Come on, Nina, let's go."

"No, you can't," said Sheely miserably.

"No? What are you going to do, call the cops? Don't bother, I'm on it," I said, pulling out my cell.

"Miles!" said Nina, her voice tense. I looked up.

Sheely was holding a pistol.

Having a gun pointed at you is not a fun time. You can feel your individual molecules struggling to get away, like your body's trying to make a hole for the bullet to pass through on its merry way. I tried not to let it show on my face.

"Just calm down," I told him. "Don't do anything stupid. Quinlan's death was an accident—do you really want murder on your conscience?"

"I'm sorry Mr. Bowman. But I have no *choice*!" he said, his voice ragged. "You two are the only ones who know what happened." He clutched the pistol tighter, his knuckles whitening.

"Well, not quite," I said, looking over his left shoulder. "Whenever you're ready!"

Sheely spun to his left with a snarl. The pistol shook in his grip as he peered blindly into the shadows. So he was completely unprepared when Gary stepped out from behind the tombstone to the right and slammed his IM hockey stick down onto Sheely's outstretched arm. The gun dropped from his nerveless fingers as Nina and I ran toward him. She scrambled for the weapon, and I threw myself on Sheely.

My past experience with fighting was limited to the mosh pit at last year's **Spring Fling**, but luckily, Sheely wasn't putting up much resistance. If anything he seemed relieved that it was over. I wound up sitting on his chest as he cradled his head in his hands, sobbing. Nina approached, holding the gun gingerly by the barrel. "You're going to rot in jail," she snarled at Sheely. "And you deserve it. You killed your oldest friend and tried to cover it up!"

"Not to mention you betrayed the trust of the student body," added the Puh, his voice thick with emotion.

"Gary," I said gently, "are you crying?"

"A dean, Miles," he sobbed. "A Yale dean. How could he?"

"I'm sure the other Yale deans are paragons of virtue and wisdom," said McNeil, coming out of the darkness with Shechner.

"You get all that?" I asked.

> **Spring Fling:** A concert/all-day carnival, held the Saturday before reading week on Old Campus. It features awesome BBQs and moonbounces, and thanks to the new student activities fee, the YCC can now afford good bands, too. In 2006 it managed to snag Ben Folds *and* Ludacris.

CHAPTER SIXTEEN

Jessica held up a video camera. "Yup," she grinned. "I even got some great close-ups of you pounding on him. It's a little green from the night vision, but I think it'll be enough for the cops. Might sell pretty decently on the internet, for that matter."

McNeil looked down at the box by Silliman's grave. "So the Opal was just a prank?"

"Disappointed?" I asked.

He smiled. "Are you kidding? This is great! Protecting the gem, that was okay. Pretending to protect the gem, while secretly hoping that people tear up the campus looking for it . . . that will be better. Shechner, throw me that wild goose thing!"

"What are you doing?" I asked.

"I'm rehiding the box before the cops show up," said McNeil, putting it back in the ground and picking up my shovel. "We'll spend the rest of the year planting new clues. And this time we'll put the first one in **CCL**, where somebody's bound to stumble upon it."

"You're a credit to the university, Bowman," said Jessica. "I'll probably be working around here next year, so give me a call when you turn twenty-one. I'll stand you to a half-yard at **Richter's**."

Nina had been quiet for a while. "You okay?" I asked her softly.

"Yeah. I guess I'm a bit sad that I won't be on the cover of Archeology Monthly. Had my blouse all picked out."

CCL: Cross Campus Library, underneath Cross Campus, is being completely renovated (which is good, because it was fug-ugly). Although Sterling is the largest library, CCL contains the most-used books and has the longest hours.

Richter's: New Haven's oldest bar (founded 1858). They serve beer in giant half-yard glasses, which is a step up from the red plastic cups, but you'll have to wait till you're legal. Sorry.

"Well, I'm just glad I don't have to worry about you getting murdered anymore." I took the pistol from her and offered it to Gary. "We're going to get the police. Can you guard Sheely till we get back?"

"I got him," he said. He was still crying softly, but his voice was firm and cold. I hoped for Sheely's own sake that he didn't try to run.

"Walk slowly," huffed McNeil. "I'm still digging."

CHAPTER
Seventeen

The dorms stay open over Thanksgiving break, and since I missed my flight out answering questions at the New Haven Police Department, I decided to stay on campus and enjoy having the building (and the big-screen TV) all to myself. The Stiles Master had invited all students still in town to his place for Thanksgiving dinner, but Gary (who had no intention of leaving New Haven if it meant missing **Yale hockey**) had made me an offer I couldn't refuse.

"Happy Thanksgiving, Puh," I said, taking another bite of **Pepe's** signature pie: clam and garlic, no sauce or cheese.

"For once," he grinned at me, folding a slice in half, "we can get a table without waiting. I feel a little guilty about not eating any turkey, though."

"C'mon. If Pepe's had been around in 1621, this is what the Pilgrims would have eaten."

He shook his head. "I still don't believe a Yale dean committed a crime."

Yale Hockey: Tickets to the games, played mostly on Friday and Saturday evenings, are available for free at the bookstore. The team's usually pretty good, and the Yale rink is a very cool building known as the Whale because of its distinctive curved roof. The unofficial mascot of the hockey team is Captain Freedom, a guy from DKE who dresses up as a superhero and rides the Zamboni.

Pepe's: Pepe's, founded in 1925, is often cited as the first pizza restaurant in the United States. Many will also argue that it's the best—people actually travel in from all over the world to sample its pies. There are many who contend that archrival Sally's, about a hundred feet away, is superior.

"The police said that it turned out he was way in debt. Money does strange things to people. Even Yale deans."

For a second it looked like he was going to tear up again, but he fought it off. "So, how are you doing?" he asked.

"Great, actually," I told him. "I got a paper that I have to make up over **reading period**, but that was probably going to be the case anyway."

"You don't seem so happy. Not as happy as you should be after all of this."

I looked down at the pattern of clams on my piece of pizza. They were sort of in an unhappy-face-emoticon pattern. He was right. I wasn't quite satisfied. Even my pizza was telling me this.

"What about Nina?" he asked.

"I haven't talked to her since the police station," I said. Nina, like me, had been forced to cancel her travel plans. "But maybe it's just as well. She's still with Paul. She'll *remain* with Paul, because Paul is perfect, and *I* am not. Unless you know something I don't."

"No, just wondering," he said. "You going to eat that last slice?"

* * * * *

I was walking across the **New Haven Green** on my way back to Stiles when Nina called.

---

reading period: After classes end and before exams begin comes one week of virtually nothing. This is a test of your organizational skills. The good students will keep waking up early and studying hard. Most will goof off for a few days and then have a nervous breakdown.

New Haven Green: The ancient central lawn of the city, to the east of the Old Campus. The Puritans supposedly made it large enough to fit 100,000 people, the number they believed would be saved when Christ returned. At night, it's creepy for two reasons: (1) This was the town's original graveyard, and thousands of bodies (the exact figure is unknown, but it's presumably no more than 100,000) are still buried here, and (2) it's poorly lit. However, many will claim that you're perfectly safe out there, because anyone who sees you will assume you must be dangerously insane.

CHAPTER SEVENTEEN

"Do you feel like something's . . . not done?" she asked, as soon as I picked up.

"You too?"

"Yeah," she said. "It's weird. I just did about everything possible in my room, including backing up every file on my computer, just because I felt like something was undone. I thought maybe you knew what it was."

"Sorry," I said. "I really wish I could help you."

She was silent for a moment.

"Me too," she said. "Call me if you figure it out."

* * * * *

Back in Stiles, I sat on my bed, staring at the TV, where a Botswanan goat herder was frozen in time on **Scola**. The school was too damn quiet. Yale usually has a breathless feeling to it—thousands of brilliant people pushing themselves to the point of exhaustion to do amazing things. Every day there's shows, debates, music, and video game tournaments, all for free. (Well, the tournament might have an entry fee.) Even if you didn't have anything to do, you'd never sleep. But you do have stuff to do. You're humbled and challenged by the people you're with, to try to excel at something and make Yale a little more awesome in your own way.

My eye caught on *The Philogelos*, lying facedown on my desk. I groaned, realizing that it was now a week overdue, not to mention damaged. "Oh well,"

Scola: Scola and Scola 2 are two channels provided by the Yale cable system that show broadcasts from around the world. Even if you don't know the language, the stuff can be mesmerizing. But sometimes—well, often—the Scolas will get stuck on a single freeze-frame for days at a time, which can be kind of mesmerizing as well.

I said out loud, just to break the silence. "Might as well get my money's worth." I picked it up and flipped open the yellowed pages.

Someone needled a jokester: "I had your wife, without paying a dime." He replied: "It's my duty as a husband to couple with such a monstrosity. What made you do it?"

I kept going. Not all of them had aged so well:

An Abderite who was a eunuch had the misfortune to develop a hernia.

Ka-ching!

Then about five pages from the end, I came to this:

Knocke knocke. Who iff theyre. Merry, looke inne the falfe bottomme. P.S.: I, Cooper, declare thys to be the moft excellent of my jestes.

I read it a few times and then closed the book. "Well," I said to myself. "Next time, I'll make sure to finish the book **before I write a paper on it**."

I picked up my phone and called Nina.

"I know what it is," I said. "How fast can you get over here? And dress warm."

* * * * *

"Sorry Ben," I murmured, as I dug up his grave for the second time.

"What are you doing?" Nina said, holding the flashlight above me.

---

before I write a paper on it: Most incoming Yalies start out with the adorable idea of reading everything they're assigned. They quickly learn that academia is all about being able to determine what you really need to read, how much, and how closely. And while writing a paper without having read the entire book you're supposed to be analyzing is not recommended, it's not uncommon. Moreover, it makes our twist ending possible.

I hadn't explained to her our purpose in being out here, largely because I was afraid I was wrong. After a couple minutes, I hit the box and worked it out of the packed soil. It took me a minute to find the false bottom—they really knew how to work with wood back then. But I finally slid a plank down and to the side, and sure enough there was a small compartment, containing something wrapped in velvet.

"What's that?" she gasped. "Miles . . . what *is* that?"

"It was the one last thing we had to do," I said, pulling out the bundle.

"No. It can't be."

"Here," I said, setting the bundle in Nina's hand and taking the flashlight. "You do the honors."

She glanced at me, wide-eyed, then pulled the strings apart that wound around the velvet. It fell open to reveal a gem. It was huge, about the size of an egg. It was smooth and not quite round. Even in the darkness, it somehow found a way to sparkle.

"Cooper was clever," I said. "He wanted to make sure that if anyone ever did find the Opal, at least it would be someone with both the dedication to solve the clues and the sense of humor to actually read the jokebook. Which I finally did tonight."

She was silent for a moment, looking at the massive gem in her palm.

"You could have come here alone," she said. "You could have claimed this all for yourself."

"Where's the fun in that?" I asked. As I spoke, I felt my face flushing a deep, revealing red. Luckily, it was too dark for her to see. I hoped. The graveyard seemed ridiculously quiet. I felt like we were alone in the world with the Opal and the ghost of James Fenimore Cooper grinning at us from behind a mausoleum.

Neither of us seemed to know what to say after that, so we filled in the hole and started to walk back rapidly, our steps magically falling in time with each other. I was clutching the Opal so tightly that I was half afraid I was going to break it.

Nina cleared her throat. "So I had a long talk with Paul today."

Something about the tone of her voice made my ears perk up. "One of *those* long talks?" I said, trying not to sound excited.

She nodded. "Believe it or not, I interrupted his **blue booking** for next semester. But he took it well. If anyone's going to handle a breakup perfectly, it's him. I think he was kind of expecting it. I think he knew that there was another guy."

"Oh," I said, silver-tongued devil that I am. Looking down at the Opal, I swallowed once, then put it in my jacket pocket and reached out to take her hand.

"So?" she said, breaking the silence and erupting into a huge grin. "Admit it, you're glad we did this."

"What part am I glad about?" I fake-grumbled, matching her grin with my own. "Someone's going to claim that rock you've got there. They'll never let us keep it. So what does that leave us? The part where we almost got expelled, or the part where we almost got shot?"

"How about when you saw me naked?"

"I wasn't looking!" I insisted.

"Come on . . ."

"No, I wasn't! I was too worried about the hunt."

We hurried on in silence for a minute, and then Nina pulled me to a halt.

"I looked at *you*," she said.

---

blue booking: The annual book of Yale's course offerings, delivered each August. In the first couple weeks of the semester, Yalies spend many hours "blue booking," and even attend "blue book parties." The online version of the blue book is far more useful. For instance, you can search for all the courses with *pirate* in the description that meet on Tuesdays. Arrr.

About the Authors

Matthew Belinkie, TC '02, briefly ran a Yale-based detective agency. He wrote a paper on video game audio that got him quoted in the *Washington Post*. He was banned for life from WYBC. His portrayal of the titular role in the Yale Children's Theater production of *You're a Good Man Charlie Brown* was hailed by the *Herald* as "pulled off with ample 'aww shucks!' charm." He currently works for ESPN in New York, and has written a number of very funny screenplays that nobody will buy.

Jordan Stokes, ES '03, was preceded at Yale by his father, grandfather, uncles, great uncles, and his great-great . . . (etc.) granduncle Jonathan Edwards. Much to the chagrin of his illustrious ancestors, he decided to major in music, and once received a D in a Credit-D-Fail art history course. Today, Jordan makes photocopies for the New York Youth Symphony, and is hard at work on *Search for the Eli Opal 2: the Curse of Zombie Silliman*!

SPARKCOLLEGE

ALSO AVAILABLE FROM SPARKCOLLEGE

Great College Guides
$12.95 EACH

A great college is a great fit. Our *Great College* series highlights schools that excel at developing students' potential and values, featuring programs that create a more engaging, hands-on approach to learning.

NOW AVAILABLE

57 Great Colleges in California and Nevada
1411499948

81 Great Colleges in Florida, Georgia & Alabama
1411499905

123 Great Colleges in New England
141149993X

COMING SOON

101 Great Colleges in Texas and the Southwest
1411499921

95 Great Colleges in New York
1411499913

129 Great Colleges in the Eastern Great Lakes
1411499891

103 Great Colleges in the Central Midwest
1411499840

95 Great Colleges in New Jersey and Pennsylvania
1411499867

99 Great Colleges in the Northwest and Hawaii
1411499859

97 Great Colleges in the Upper Midwest
1411499875

10 Things You Gotta Know
$7.95 EACH

This series is for high school students in the process of applying to college. Each subject-specific book is filled with quickly digestible chunks of information as well as tons of top 10 lists for vital facts at a glance.

10 Things You Gotta Know: College Application Essays
1411403495

10 Things You Gotta Know: Paying for College
1411403517

10 Things You Gotta Know: Your First Year of College
1411403525

10 Things You Gotta Know: Choosing a College
1411403509

College Planner
$14.95 1411402804

Your all-in-one guide for choosing and applying to college includes: Spiral-bound college-search guide, college-visit journal, U.S. map of 1,000 colleges, and pockets for applications and notes.

Treasure Schools
$12.95 1411499883

These are the little-known schools that offer truly exceptional educational opportunities—America's college gems that students need to know about.

Find Your Best College Fit!